Whisper in the Waves

Murder in Plymouth Harbor

An Eye in the Sky Mystery

Dianne Hunt Smith

Briley & Baxter Publications | Plymouth, Massachusetts

ISBN: 978-1-961978-64-5.

Book Design: Amy Deyerle-Smith

I would like to dedicate this book to two special people who left us much too early, and whom I think of often. I will always hold a place in my heart for you Thom, and JW as well. I know you're both among the brightest stars shining above me when I look up at night. Cheers. I miss you both.

1

PACIFIC OCEAN 1840

LINCOLN WOODWORTH'S FROZEN hands shook as he lit the greasy oil lantern inside the dank, dingy cabin he shared with his brother, Benjamin, on board the bark Orion. Originally setting sail from New Bedford, Massachusetts, the *Orion* had recently left the port of San Francisco on a whaling expedition that planned to culminate at the Arctic Circle before eventually returning home to Massachusetts.

Within seconds, the flame ignited, and a dancing yellow glow overtook the cabin. Quickly sliding the rusty iron bar across the cabin door to lock it, Linc began peeling off his soaking wet, nearly frozen clothing with his fingers numb and white, as his entire body began to shake uncontrollably. He quickly dried himself and pulled on a dry pair of woolen breeches, heavy stockings, and a thick fur cape to help warm himself. His memories racing, he couldn't shake the horrible images away. Not wanting the other crew members to overhear him or try to console him, he curled himself into a ball on the narrow bunk beneath the one his brother Ben slept on, burrowed deeper under the heavy, soiled blankets, and the twenty-year-old young man began to sob.

The sodden vessel groaned loudly and lurched forward, the floorboards creaking as Linc tried desperately to erase the images flooding his thoughts, his body continuing to convulse from the cold, hidden deep beneath the heavy, musty layers in his bunk.

Hours later, Linc awoke with a start and gradually became fully awake. His mind began to replay the tragic scene that had taken place hours earlier while chasing down the largest whale they had followed to date. Unsteadily swinging his legs over the side of the bunk and holding his head in his hands, Linc sat motionless as the ship rolled and forged ahead through the heavy surf, his brain trying to form the words he would use to relay the unbearable news.

A raging anger surged through the shaky, grief-stricken man as he stood and stared out the round, salt encrusted porthole for several long minutes. He pulled out the well-worn chair in front of the small writing desk he and his brother had shared and slowly slid open the desk's only drawer. He located his quill pen, tiny ink bottle, and tablet for writing. He regretfully began his letter:

Dearest Mother

It is with tremendous sadness that I write to you from my expedition since departing San Francisco. I wish with all my heart that I did not have to pen this letter to you, and I pray it shall reach you more quickly than my last correspondence.

Today, whilst engaging in the chase of an extremely large and violent humpback whale, our vessel encountered a storm with lightning and heaving winds. Giant waves crashed over the bow while we tried with great vigor to stop the huge beast from thrashing and entangling our boat in the lines.

We could scarcely see through the rain and fog while the wind howled about, and it seemed our boat had broken apart near the bow due to the massive waves.

We felt a rush of hope when another whaling ship appeared through the thick fog. We waved and hollered frantically as they approached because we recognized the ship and thought, Finally! Aid has arrived!...

2024 PLYMOUTH HARBOR, Massachusetts

WILL CLARKE TURNED the ignition key, the diesel engine sputtering and coughing before kicking in and fully turning over. Black smoke belched and puffed upward from the stern of *Dolphin II* as Will slowly chugged in reverse, backing her from the slip at the Plymouth Town Pier. Wiping his greasy hands on his jeans, he peered out through the pitted, grimy window of the wheelhouse aboard the top level of the whale watch tour boat and carefully inched his way around the smaller boats moored in the harbor.

It was early, just an hour or so after sunrise, and the harbor's morning traffic hadn't really started except for a few lobster boats preparing to head out to check their traps. Will loved the early mornings on the water and enjoyed the calm and quiet before the day trippers scheduled to hunt for whales started arriving and lining up on the dock. The itinerary for the upcoming day was full, and Will silently hoped his boat would continue behaving and that Dolphin *II's* engine problems were behind him.

Dolphin II had been experiencing unusual engine issues, and Will had spent most of the previous evening working on the boat in its slip until well after dark. He had done the majority of the required mechanical work himself, but eventually hunger and fatigue caught up with him. He left the pier around 9 pm and returned to his apartment to have dinner, and planned to come back early the next morning to take the boat out for a test ride.

Will had purchased the tour boat three summers earlier when a local captain /owner decided he had spent enough years hauling people out into the chilly Cape Cod Bay to hopefully see a whale or two. Will had worked seven years on the boat, first as a galley worker, then a deckhand, a first mate, and eventually worked his way up to earning his captain's license and piloting the boat. When his former boss retired, he offered Will a chance to buy it from him and make payments towards eventually owning it. Will took him up on his offer and finally finished paying it off over the previous winter. He spent most of the spring preparing for the upcoming tourist season, getting the boat in good mechanical condition before they started the daily trips out to Stellwagen Bank, where whales are most frequently spotted.

"So far so good," Will thought to himself as he continued slowly heading out of the harbor, past the jetty towards "Bug Light," a local landmark off the tip of Long Beach in Plymouth.

The sky was a clear, bright blue, and the sun sparkled off the water as Will scanned left and right, carefully entering the open water and accelerating his boat.

While listening closely for engine sounds that he hoped he wouldn't hear, Will gradually eased into the throttle and proceeded into the wide-open expanse of the Atlantic Ocean. After heading out for approximately half a mile before turning back towards the harbor, he spotted another vessel off his port side approaching at what appeared to be a rapid speed.

Squinting from the sun glare, he pulled his sunglasses down and tried to identify the approaching boat.

"Oh crap," Will muttered "It's him again. Look at that fool and the wake he's leaving!" Just as Will said the words, the boat turned enough so he could see the name on the bow clearly. The vessel slowed slightly and appeared to be approaching him. As salt water sprayed and wake churned all around his bow, Will slowed his vessel down and waited to see exactly where *Velella* was headed.

The other whale watching boat gradually slowed down and approached *Dolphin II* as Will sat idling in the swells, wondering what the other captain might be doing.

"What the hell is *he* doing here?" Will said aloud. "Nice start to my day... seeing that moron. I wonder what he wants?"

The *Velella* slowed enough to get near Dolphin *II*, both boats bobbing up and down as Will angrily slid his window open and stuck his head out to yell at the captain of the other boat.

"What!?? What the hell do you want? And keep your distance!!" You're too damn close!"

The other captain reached his arm out the window and flicked his cigarette in Will's direction, looking out with an exaggerated smirk and throwing his head back to bellow a loud, artificial laugh. His baseball cap turned backwards and long, greasy hair trailing down his stained t-shirt hardly gave Patrick Walsh a distinguished look behind the wheel.

"No dude," Patrick yelled over the two droning diesels. "*You're* too close!! Too close to getting in *my* way and pissing *me* off! Last trip out, you totally encroached on my area. I had a full charter, and you moved right in! Do it again, dude, and I promise it won't be pretty!!"

With that, Patrick pointed his finger out the window directly at Will and clearly mouthed several swears before putting his boat in gear and chugging back towards the harbor.

Will spat out the window and watched *Velella* and Patrick Walsh disappear, wishing he had spoken up during the brief confrontation, even if just to stand his ground and let the well-established bully know he couldn't push him around. Will knew he hadn't *really* encroached on his area on his last whale watch- at least not much- and now he felt a brief wave of regret washing over him.

"I'll have to be more careful," Will thought as he slipped into gear and turned his boat back towards land. He replayed his last tour out and tried to remember how it truly went down, when he and the *Velella* got a little too close. both boats trying to get their customers nearest to the whale spotted on the tail end of their trip.

Not feeling responsible for all the blame in this case, Will figured both captains pushed the boundary a bit too far. They both knew better, but sometimes egos get in the way, and competing companies want to be number one in the area. Unfortunately for Will, there were currently three whale watch tour companies along "his" section of coast. Although his was the only company based in Plymouth, the two others located in Sandwich (a coastal town south of Plymouth at the start of Cape Cod) and Duxbury (a coastal town north of Plymouth) respectively, now claimed their fair amount of business from the local tourist industry. With only one boat, Will felt the pinch and wanted to maintain his foothold on the Plymouth tourist trade. He had recently started to sense competition from other companies and inwardly vowed to keep what he had worked so hard for, not letting anyone get in his way.

Pushing the throttle forward, *Dolphin II* inched its way back towards Plymouth Harbor and Will mentally prepared for the upcoming day trip. He was happy with how the engine was sounding and running, figuring the ticket fees for the group he had scheduled later this week would cover the cost of parts he needed to purchase for necessary repairs.

"Not much of a profit today, I guess," Will thought. "But at least I'm running. Could be worse."

Slowing down while entering the harbor, Will approached his spot at the pier (which he paid handsomely for) and got a hand tying up securely. Before climbing down from the wheelhouse and heading to his pickup truck, he looked around to see if Patrick Walsh was anywhere in sight.

Patrick's boat looked as if he was headed into Plymouth Harbor, although his business was based out of the marina in Sandwich. He had probably gone to refuel when he sped away, and Will really didn't want to have another run-in with him at the dock.

Will had known Patrick since high school, although they were never what he considered "friends," rather two guys who knew each other from hanging out at parties and sports. These days, Will occasionally ran into "Trick" (as he was usually called) at one of the local pubs where they both played in a darts league. Will didn't usually go out of his way to avoid Trick, but since their chat earlier on the water, he thought it was probably best to keep a low profile around the guy.

Trick earned his nickname, not only as a derivative of his name, Patrick, but also thanks to a long history of hustling bar patrons into innocently playing darts. Because he had exceptional skills with dart throwing, Trick was able to win most games with his pinpoint accuracy. He usually played for money, and the most gullible or greedy victims often fell prey to his "trick," leaving the bar with their money and their pride nowhere to be found. Trick derived great pleasure from the monetary victories and showed off his impressive throwing skills to any patrons in the bar.

Will checked on his boat lines one final time and locked the flimsy door to the upper deck wheelhouse. Security was loose around the pier, and there were usually a few boat break-ins over the summer. Luckily, nothing major has happened to any of the boats belonging to people Will considered his friends. Most boat owners kept an eye out for each other, and the word traveled fast if somebody with questionable intent was spotted hanging around the marina or pier. Will was glad he'd never had to deal with a theft or damage since owning *Dolphin II,* and he wanted to keep it that way.

3

JONATHAN WOODWORTH SHOVED the throttle forward as he sat in the captain's chair, high inside the air-conditioned wheelhouse. *Merlin,* his almost new, fifty-six-foot whale watching tour boat, sliced easily through the rolling swells and only tipped a bit when Jon gunned it and pointed her bow towards the open water. Grinning broadly, Jon adjusted his best pair of Ray-Bans into position and continued his ride towards the horizon for several minutes until he gradually cut back the throttle and gently arced back around towards his starting point. The *Merlin* purred and responded perfectly, just as Jon knew she would. He thought she was worth every penny he'd spent.

Last summer, Jon unexpectedly inherited a very large sum of money and promptly decided he would purchase a whale watching tour boat in his coastal hometown of Duxbury, Massachusetts. The Woodworth family had a prosperous seafaring history within the town, and when Jon inherited the money from his grandfather, a lifelong Duxbury resident, retaining the necessary permits wasn't much of a problem. Ancestors in Jon's family ran a very successful whaling enterprise in the 1800s and built numerous stately sea captains' homes along the coastline in Duxbury. The family prospered over the years and subsequently owned valuable parcels of land all over town. The endowments the Woodworth family had made to the community- and the fact that key people turned a blind eye when it came to licensing protocols- enabled Jon to obtain permits quickly and begin his whale watching venture with barely a ripple of delay or red tape.

This year would be Jon's first full summer season. He had devised a definitive plan: have a prosperous season piloting his own boat and running the new business *his way*. Jon's father had offered to help him with the accounting and business aspects of the new company, but Jon had flatly refused his help and boasted that he would be successful without his father's interference. The "well-to-do" Woodworth family quietly retreated, and Jon mysteriously secured a coveted spot at the town pier to dock his new boat. He didn't fully consider the other two whale watching companies as stiff competition. Will Clarke in Plymouth had only one boat, and Trick Walsh in Sandwich wasn't the brightest bulb on the tree (in Jon's estimation). He hoped to squeeze out both Will and Trick Walsh's operations by next season and possibly purchase himself a second, and maybe even a third, tour boat. The plan kept getting bigger! Full steam ahead.

After slowing down to enter Snug Harbor, Jon maneuvered back into his slip and docked. He locked up his baby and sauntered down the bobbing dock towards the parking lot.

"It's gonna be one helluva summer," Jon said happily to himself as he headed towards his Range Rover, occupying two reserved spots in the marina's parking lot. A townie had their privileges!

"And nobody's gonna get in my way!" He laughed aloud before hopping in his vehicle, leaving a cloud of dust and gravel behind him as he tore away.

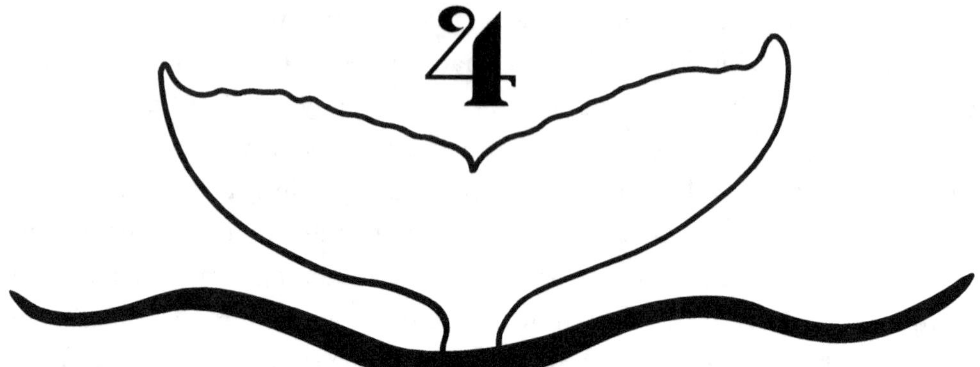

4

WILL PULLED OUT a stool at The Depot, a local pub where he sometimes spent his free time hanging out with friends and playing in a local darts league. The food was pretty decent, and Will knew a lot of the fishermen in town who regularly stopped by for a beer or two. It was busy for a weeknight, and Will figured he would have a bite to eat, down a couple of Sam Adams, and get ready to play in the dart tournament starting at 8:00pm.

He ordered his food and sat watching the muted TV positioned above the busy bar, not really paying attention to the baseball game occupying the screen. He wondered if Trick would show up at the bar later to play darts. He was on an opposing team and didn't always show up in time to play. Glancing around, Will didn't notice him anywhere in sight and felt somewhat relieved. He just wanted to have a quiet night and go home- hopefully after winning the dart tournament. The pub was getting noisy, and more patrons started trickling in. Will kept an eye out for Trick and waited patiently for his burger to arrive.

Will hoped their exchange on the water earlier today wouldn't be a lingering issue for Trick, but he still wondered. He had seen Trick's nasty temper one night when he had a few too many beers and started bullying a patron, so Will decided to keep a low profile so as not to tick him off tonight.

Halfway through his burger and first Sam Adams, Will spotted Trick at the far end of the bar, clapping his buddies on the back, and quickly throwing back two shots before the dart tournament started in half an hour. Trick was loud and boisterous and knew almost everyone in the pub. Will silently wished he wasn't in the dart league with him. Yes, he was a damn good dart thrower, probably the best in the league, but the guy was certainly a loose cannon, and Will wanted to stay on his good side whenever possible.

As he finished dinner, Will saw Trick working his way along the opposite side of the bar. Keeping an eye on Trick while also trying to appear to be watching the TV, Will stole a glance in his direction and was inwardly shocked when Trick pointed his finger directly at him, as if pointing a gun, and pulled an imaginary trigger in his direction. He grinned boldly while staring at Will with his oddly spaced front teeth and gave him a quick, exaggerated wink.

Will instantly looked away, feeling his face flush and hoping nobody else noticed what had just gone down across the bar. He stood up, put his money down, and moved away from the bar towards the dartboard area and the guys on his darts team. He got the hint.

The dart tournament went as usual. Will's team came in second in their group, and they all won a free beer at the end of their round.

"No cash prize tonight," Will thought, disappointed that he was going home without prize money. "Maybe next week... At least the free beer was a happily welcomed second-place prize.

While standing at the bar to claim his runner-up prize, Will heard a commotion at the other end of the pub. Two other teams were finishing their final rounds, and Will was not surprised to hear Trick's voice rising above the rest. Hearing swearing and stools rustling around, the pub patrons started to back away from two guys who were, very apparently, starting a heated argument. Will looked over in the direction of the raised voices and noticed that Trick Walsh, and somebody who looked similar to Jonathan Woodworth, were shoving each other back and forth in front of the dartboard. Most of the crowd previously watching the dart games had moved away from the pair as they began to circle each other. They were insulting each other back and forth, but Will couldn't understand what they were saying over the noise in the bar. A few of the darts players attempted to separate Trick and Jon and move them out of the pub. Jon broke free and started heading for the exit on his own, turning around to confront Trick before he stormed out the door.

"Okay, A-Hole," Jon spat out, glaring at Trick. "You may have won the battle, but I'll win the war. Watch your back, dude. I fight fire with fire." You're on my list."

The door slammed behind him as Jon stomped out. Trick looked uneasily around the almost silent pub while the other patrons began to laugh nervously, waiting for his response. "Oooooh, watch me tremble, I'm soooo afraid," Trick says in a falsetto voice.

He put his empty beer mug back on the bar, paid his tab, and walked out. The din at the bar resumed and everybody went back to what they were doing.

Will chugged the remainder of his beer as he was getting ready to leave, and wondered exactly what Trick and Jon were fighting about.

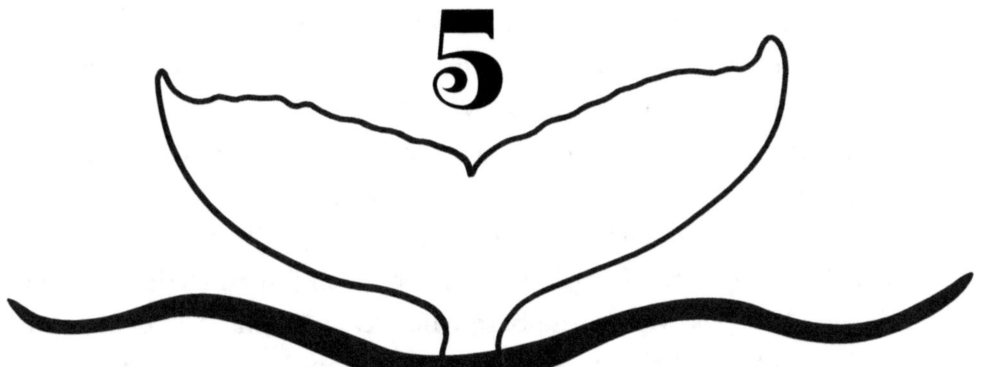

5

WILL LEFT THE Depot and walked down the alley that ran between the bar and hair salon next door. This shortcut was used by most patrons to access the rear parking lot quickly and without walking down the main street. It was a beautiful, early June evening, and the air was turning warmer with each passing day. Will looked forward to the upcoming season and was excited about the new crew he had hired to help kick it off. He planned on scheduling a get-together so the crew could meet before the season officially started, hoping they would all get along with one another. A happy crew can make a world of difference, and Will felt that he had a giant stroke of good luck when a former employee of Jon Woodworth's contacted him on Facebook, looking for a job.

Will met up with Jack White, showed him his boat, and instantly liked him. He was impressed with Jack's resume and qualifications and hired him as Chief Mate on the spot. Jack seemed like a decent guy with lots of boating experience and a quiet demeanor, which Will found refreshing. Hiring teens and college-aged kids saved a few bucks, but Will learned they generally weren't the most dedicated employees, nor the most reliable. He wasn't sure what caused the rift between Jon and Jack, but he still thought he would be a great addition to his staff and hoped his hunch was correct.

At the edge of the parking lot, Will heard raised voices and could see two people under a streetlight in the tree limb shadows. While standing very close together, one pulled back and tried to grip the other in a headlock.

They began to scuffle, and both fell to the ground out of Will's line of sight. He could hear them swearing and breathing heavily as they rolled on the ground, pummeling each other and continuing to fight.

Standing in the shadows at the edge of the gravel parking lot, hidden behind an overgrown row of hedges, Will silently watched as the two men stood up again and grappled some more. One man punched the other hard enough for him to fall backwards, and Will could hear the man on the receiving end of the punch hit the ground and groan loudly. He was sure this was a continuation of the fight in the pub between Jon and Trick, but Will couldn't tell who was who in the barely lit area, just that one person was clearly winning the fight. With one man down and the other standing unsteadily, breathing heavily as he loomed over the lump on the ground, Will watched as the winner turned and slowly disappeared into the darkness of the far corner of the parking lot. The form on the ground slowly rose to his feet, brushed himself off, and stood unmoving in the dark shadows. After a brief pause, under the partial shadow from the streetlight, the second man disappeared down the partially lit sidewalk, and Will waited a moment before continuing to his own pickup at the far end of the lot.

"Holy crap," Will said to himself as he hurried towards his pickup, hoping both men left the area for good. He was sure of who he saw fighting, but he was unable to see who had clearly won that round. One of those two guys took a beating, and Will didn't want to let anyone know that he was a witness.

Hopping in his truck, starting it up, and driving home, Will was shaken up by the evening's events. It was clear that Trick and Jon had animosity between them, and Will vowed to stay out of all their drama. He had a busy summer ahead, and he didn't need to be involved in any unnecessary friction with either of the other captains. He had a single focus this summer, and it was getting his business underway and becoming the number one whale watching tour company on the South Shore. Nothing would stand in his way.

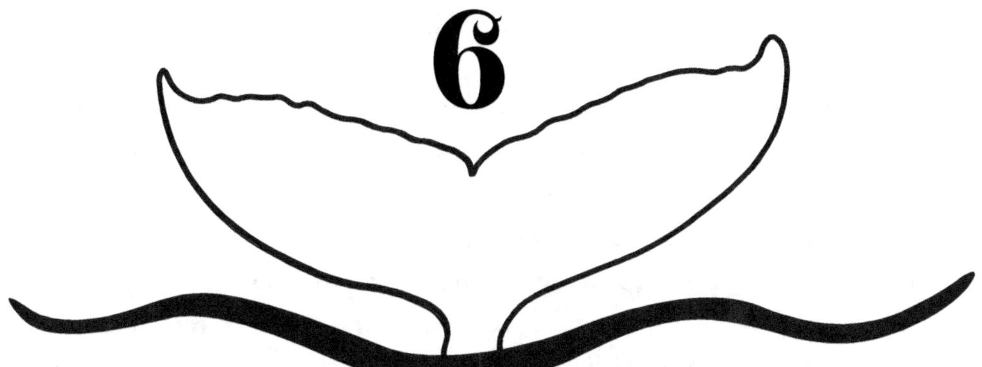

6

KAT SAT IN her pajamas and sipped her morning coffee while casually scrolling online through the pages of *The Journal*, her town's local weekly newspaper. The weather had finally taken a turn towards the warmer side, and freelance photographer, Kat MacIntyre Finley, was looking forward to a peaceful summer mixed with just a little bit of work. The luxury of sleeping late and staying in her pajamas was a rare one, and Kat was relishing the balmy, quiet morning, enjoying her coffee, and catching up on local news on her computer.

Skimming the headlines as they flashed by, Kat stopped abruptly, then scrolled back to get to the beginning of the featured story. The article that caught her eye was titled: *Holiday Break-In at Plymouth Whaling Museum: Historical Artifacts Stolen Include Antique Whaling Harpoon.*

"Oh my gosh," Kat muttered to herself. "Wow! That's awful news for the museum...and kind of creepy."

She read the entire article and was saddened to learn that the museum had several of its most popular whaling artifacts stolen in the Memorial Day weekend break-in, and the police currently had no strong suspects as they started their investigation. The article also stated that several pieces of valuable scrimshaw, depicting the whaling era, had also been found missing after the robbery. The article concluded with comments from the Chief of Police in Plymouth who confirmed that they were actively following several potential leads and would keep the public posted on updates.

The article also included several photographs of the stolen objects. Kat peered closer at the whaling harpoon that had disappeared and imagined the nearly impossible task of impaling a multi-ton whale using only human strength.

"That thing must be incredibly sharp," Kat thought to herself. "I can't imagine hoisting it up and throwing it far and hard enough to even reach the whale, never mind injure the whale."

The first photograph showed the harpoon from several angles: the sharp points on the two barbs appearing like giant, rusted fangs.

The next photo showed six pieces of round scrimshaw, made from whales' teeth and bones, which had images depicting whalers and whales etched onto their flat, matte pearl-colored surfaces from almost two hundred years ago. Several of the pieces had two initials inscribed on the back in black ink and a fancy script. Like coins from the sea, these ornate pieces became highly valued, and gifts of scrimshaw were always welcomed. Sailors spent months at sea, passing the hours by creating intricately etched pieces and other artifacts made from the bones of the whales they caught.

Kat shuddered and took one last look at the items before shutting off her laptop and slipping off her stool where she sat reading on the kitchen island. Her little pup, Dash, was curled in a ball, snoozing directly below her, and gazed up sleepily when she stood up. Dash was a rescue dog Kat and her husband Drew had adopted the year before, and he had become her constant companion, both when she traveled for work and when she was home alone. Dash possessed an uncanny ability to sense subtle energies well before Kat could. This had served them both well during their escapades in the past. Kat knew she and Drew had chosen a one-in-a-million little pup to join their family. He was the perfect fit.

Kat and Dash once worked together to help solve a family mystery and develop the start of a powerful, mysterious bond. Included in this triangle of sleuths was Quinn MacIntyre, Kat's long-deceased ancestor, whose aid was instrumental in helping Kat understand her mediumship gift and uncover the family secret.

Through a series of "meetings" or interactions, Kat and Quinn (aka Mac) were able to open both ends of a time passage (both "here" and "on the other side") through which they can communicate with one another and help each other with the different tasks each were destined to complete on their respective sides.

When Kat, Dash, and Mac team up, mysteries can be solved using the special talents all three possess.

Kat thought about the break-in and robbery at the Whaling Museum and wondered who would do such a thing, and why? The items that were stolen seemed to be specifically chosen, in the sense that many other larger pieces of scrimshaw were left untouched, and the display of ancient whaling harpoons was missing only one weapon, apparently handpicked out of the entire collection. When she read this information online, Kat intuitively felt as if the thief or thieves showed deliberate intent when they took the specific items. But why?

Kat felt badly that the museum had suffered the loss, but also found it interesting that she had been chosen by the Chamber of Commerce just the week before to do a photo shoot and article about the local whale tour boat companies and the challenges they currently face within their industry. She had been given the names of several companies currently running the whale watching tours on the South Shore of Massachusetts and had spoken with one of the young men to set up an interview on his boat.

Plymouth had a local Captain, Will Clarke, whom Kat had contacted, and he had been happy to grant her an hour or so for an interview before his charter went out. He told her he was proud of operating his own boat and would get it ready for her arrival the following week. She planned to take pictures inside and out of the craft and take notes on the (hopefully) interesting stories Capt. Will could relay to her about his days following and searching for whales. The interview was set for early on Saturday morning, and Kat was looking forward to her trip out on *Dolphin II*. After her interview with Will, she had been invited to join the morning boat tour out to Stellwagen Bank in search of whales. She had readily agreed and hoped the weather would be perfect and she would have ample opportunity to get awesome pictures of any kind of whales to include in her article!

As Kat got ready to start her day, she had a nagging thought that kept popping into her head, like the snippet of a tune you can't stop humming. Something about the robbery at the Whaling Museum was bugging her. For some reason, the details surrounding the break-in were intertwining with her thoughts about her upcoming interview and photo shoot on the whale watch. They were, very obviously, two completely unrelated events, but for some reason, Kat kept experiencing feelings that were somehow connected. But how and why? No. No way.

These were two completely different scenarios. One mainly involved the past, and the other was in the future. There was no other seemingly viable connection. Still, Kat thought it was a little odd that the whaling "theme" arrived on several unconnected fronts simultaneously. Maybe after she conducted the interview on Saturday and took the boat ride to photograph the whales, she would feel reassured that there wasn't a connection between the events.

Kat was blessed with some special insights that she was still learning to navigate. These insights had started to come in handy, but she still wasn't entirely sure when to listen to those little voices and when to ignore them. Mac continued to help her learn when to tune in and when and how to disregard information flowing through her, but she was still a "work in progress!" Having mediumship skills was still very confusing, but Kat was learning to listen to her intuition. Most of it didn't make sense to her. She also kept thinking about the picture of the harpoon that was stolen. Why would someone steal just that item and some miscellaneous scrimshaw? Did the thief intend to hang on their wall? That thing was six feet long and dangerous! It was not like something you could easily drag around and show off to people. It would absolutely stand out in anyone's home. Kat assumed it would also be rather difficult to sell a stolen object from a museum that had been featured on television and in the newspapers. Even a pawn shop would question the exchange. The same went for the pieces of scrimshaw that had been shown on the news.

Kat decided she would focus on the upcoming photo shoot on *Dolphin II* and let the Plymouth Police worry about solving the break-in and theft.

She had an interesting job lined up for the Plymouth Chamber of Commerce's new tourism brochure, so she hoped the whales would cooperate on Saturday morning.

Except, there was one little thing Kat still couldn't stop thinking about: where would one display an 1800s whaling harpoon everyone knew was stolen?

"Oh well. I guess there's no sense in getting involved," Kat shrugged. "I just need to let it go."

She had a cool photo shoot to prepare for and if the weather cooperated, this whale watch trip promises to be a blast!

7

THE WEEK LEADING up to Kat's Saturday interview with Will Clarke was sunny, clear, and perfect boating weather. Tourists began trickling into Plymouth; the "summer people" arrived at all the coastal towns to start their annual routines of getting their cottages opened and ready, boats in the water, firepits, coolers, and refrigerators stocked.

None of the businesses in the area, including south towards Cape Cod and north towards Duxbury and Marshfield, complained about the increase in traffic and congestion on all the major roads. Post-pandemic freedom had been greeted with open arms in the beach towns that depended on tourists for income, and Plymouth was no different. Businesses opened their doors, and the day trippers arrived. The waterfront bustled with restaurants, bars, and shops, and Will booked at least one trip per day in advance for the week, grateful for the influx of business.

Patrick Walsh in Sandwich and Jon Woodworth in Duxbury also felt the happy tide of tourist money washing into their towns. Both enterprises booked daily trips and looked forward to increasing summer revenue. Every vendor and proprietor hoped the terrific weather and whale-loving tourists would continue rolling into town all summer and well into fall.

The new 2024 summer season was looking good for everyone. That was, until Jon Woodworth arrived home at his condo Wednesday evening. After cracking open a cold beer and flipping through his phone, he discovered someone had left him a rather long voicemail. Flabbergasted by the message that had been recorded, Jon swore loudly and slammed his phone down onto the granite countertop. He chugged the remainder of the beer, belched loudly, then crushed and threw the empty can into the sink. He could feel his blood beginning to boil. And then he was seething mad.

8

JON GRABBED HIS phone and shoved his way through the screen door onto the expansive back deck overlooking the country club vista he now took for granted. He leaned against the railing and punched buttons on his phone to hear to the voicemail again, this time louder.

He couldn't believe the message and wanted to listen again, more carefully this time, because his next call would be to his lawyer if necessary.

While replaying the message, Jon heard the caller identify himself as a representative from NOAA (National Oceanic and Atmospheric Administration; the federal sea monitoring agency). He was calling regarding an anonymous complaint they had received, concerning Jon's whaling boat and interactions that had supposedly taken place out on the water this past week. He requested that Jon please call his office first thing in the morning, as they had to schedule a hearing date. He continued with his message to leave contact information and a website for Jon to review. The representative then recommended Jon re-educate himself on NOAA's hearing process for handling maritime infractions and the applicable laws, which may or may not have been broken by him or someone operating his vessel.

Jon listened to the message twice, then stood quietly staring out across the fairway behind his condo for a moment, trying to figure out who the hell would turn him into NOAA. Fuming on the inside, his hands were clenched into trembling fists, and he was trying very hard to control his emotions. He vowed out loud that some S.O.B. was going to pay royally for this crap, and if he could find out who dropped the dime, he would definitely make them regret it. Was it a tourist who didn't like how he handled the whales, or was it someone closer who had something to gain by bad-mouthing his business?

Either way, Jon would play the game. But he intended to win. One way or the other.

9

KAT AWOKE EARLY on Saturday morning and was excited about the up-coming boat trip she had planned for later that day. She was looking forward to her tour of *Dolphin II* and her interview with Will Clarke as well. On the phone, he seemed like a really nice guy who was trying hard to keep his business humming along and didn't mind the hard work involved in making it happen. The weather was perfect: clear blue skies and just a hint of a breeze. Kat imagined she couldn't have picked a better day while she sipped her coffee and enjoyed the quiet morning sitting on her back deck. Dash hopped up on the end of the lounge chair, circled twice, and curled up, patiently awaiting his breakfast. As usual, he stayed close to Kat, always ready to participate in any adventure that might become part of his day. Ever since he came to live with Drew and Kat, Dash had displayed a keen ability to sense and often locate unseen energies. Kat often relied on Dash's reaction to a location to determine if any spirit-related energies might be attempting to communicate with her. Kat knew Dash (all 22 pounds of the wiry little rescue dog mix) usually tapped into what was happening around them well before she did. He was the perfect companion pup. Kat considered bringing him along for the photo shoot, but changed her mind when she envisioned the crowded boat, the boisterous tourists, and the potential for him to be-come overwhelmed. No, she decided, her little buddy would stay home to-day, inside where it was cool and where no harm could come to him, while she got to work. She'd be home by midafternoon and hopefully will have taken some great whale pictures as well as some interesting boat shots for the promo brochure.

Kat finished her coffee, fed Dash breakfast, and slipped into the shower. Gathering photo gear that she had put into a neat pile by the front door the night before, she loaded up the Jeep and prepared to head to Plymouth Town Pier. Dash was snoozing on his bed since breakfast had been served. He'd taken a spin outdoors and investigated the entire yard before doing his business. He somehow sensed he wasn't going with Kat on this trip, so he settled in for a nap until she returned home later in the day.

Drew was away, working on a project off the coast of Vancouver, British Columbia. He had become a much sought-after naturalist since publishing his most recent book. He and Kat both enjoyed their respective careers, and Drew looked forward to spending his free time with Kat and Dash whenever he got home. His current work schedule included two weeks at home, followed by two weeks in Canada at various sites. Kat didn't mind being home alone: she had Dash who was great company, she was busy with photo shoots of her own, and it gave her time to arrange a balanced social life with her friends and colleagues. She and Drew took wonderful, relaxing vacations together and often mixed work with pleasure when traveling. Kat loved being a photographer and most days enjoyed her job immensely. Looking ahead, she fully expected today to be no different.

10

PULLING INTO THE large parking lot at Plymouth Town Pier, Kat noticed there weren't many cars in the coveted spots this beautiful Saturday morning. It was still rather early, only a little before 8:00 am, the time she and Will had agreed to meet on his boat. She unloaded her camera bag from the Jeep, rolled down the windows a little to let the heat escape, and hoisted her canvas tote bag over one shoulder and camera bag over the other. Will had told her to walk down the A Pier ramp towards *Dolphin II* and come aboard. He said he would most likely be upstairs in the wheelhouse, so he may not hear her arrival, but it was fine to come up the stairs and meet him up top. He would be expecting her, and they could conduct the interview there. From there, he would take her on a tour of the boat for photos before the patrons arrived for their day trip.

It was relatively quiet around the town pier as Kat looked down at Plymouth Harbor from the parking lot. Many fishing and pleasure boats were moored in the harbor and docked at the piers, but foot traffic was quiet, except for a few fishermen loading up for the day. The seagulls were flying back and forth overhead, screeching their morning tunes while they scavenged for food scraps. The sun was getting hot overhead, and an occasional breeze ruffled the flag flying on the Harbormaster's little hut. Kat pulled her Red Sox cap down tightly, adjusted her ponytail, and her Oakleys. She was finally off to meet Capt. Will and see some whales! How exciting!

As she was working her way along the ramp leading down to the docks, Kat spotted *Dolphin II* near the far end of the longest pier. She didn't see anyone on board as she approached the ramp leading onto the boat, but wasn't surprised as Capt. Will said he would most likely be upstairs in the wheelhouse. Kat walked up the ramp, stepped onto the main deck of the tidy tour boat, and glanced around to locate the ladder (boat talk for stairs) that led to the upper deck. Once she spotted the swinging door that led upstairs, Kat readjusted her bags on each shoulder and pushed her way through. Looking upwards toward the dark, steep passageway, Kat saw something that appeared to be propping open the door at the top of the stairs. She couldn't tell exactly what it was, but as she ascended closer to the top steps, she realized that something seemed wrong. Very wrong. The wooden end of a long, whaling harpoon was indeed propping open the door at the top step, but the ghastly sight at the other end of the harpoon was what instantly shocked and revolted her. Through the partially open door, she saw Capt. Will sprawled on the floor of the wheelhouse. Thankfully, before she could take another step through the door, she froze as she felt her heart begin to pound wildly in her chest, and both bags slid off her shoulders. Her legs instantly felt like rubber; she was mesmerized and completely numbed by the sight before her. Splayed out on the floor next to the pilot's seat was Capt. Will Clarke, on his back, pinned to the floor with a large wood and iron whaling harpoon sticking out of his chest at a ghastly angle. His promising future was drained from him, pooling beneath his lifeless body. Unable to look away from the gruesome sight before her, but not wanting to look *at* it, Kat became faint, then hastily fumbled in her tote bag for her phone. With trembling hands, trying desperately not to hyperventilate, she dialed 911. She looked around the wheelhouse, still in total disbelief at the hideous manner of death, and saw no real signs of a struggle.

"Holy crap...Oh my God!!" Kat gasps out loud. Frozen in place, she puts her hand to her mouth to stifle a scream. "What the HELL??! Poor Captain Will! I can't believe this..." She closed her eyes to wash the image away and a wave of nausea crashed over her. She needed to get outside and find fresh air. Fast.

After reaching the local police and describing the scene she had just discovered, Kat carefully backed out of the wheelhouse and slowly descended the stairs to *Dolphin II's* main deck. She felt lightheaded and was very careful not to touch anything, realizing that she had just stumbled into a very violent and grisly crime scene. Once outside, she sat down, a bit unsteadily, on a plastic seat bolted to the main deck. Before she could faint, she took several deep breaths to calm herself. She fished out a bottle of water from her tote bag and took a long gulp. Her throat felt dry and hoarse when she called the police. She could barely croak out the words to the dispatcher. The boat rocked gently back and forth, as small waves rippled through the harbor and the wail of sirens in the distance worked their way towards the waterfront crime scene. Kat knew the entire pier area would soon be roped off. The police had asked her to stay at the scene, as they wanted to interview her as soon as possible. She gingerly walked down the gangway to disembark the boat and wait for the police. Kat stared out across the harbor waiting for the police to arrive and wondered, who could have done such a horrific thing to poor Will Clarke?

The summer season was just beginning, and now it looked as if there was one less whale watching company competing on the waterfront. At least for the time being.

When she replayed the gruesome scene in her mind, she just couldn't shake the thought that the impaled harpoon resembled a giant dart, and Will Clarke had become the bullseye.

With slow, careful steps, Kat approached a wooden bench located on the main pier and sat down. She closed her eyes and took several, deliberate, deep breaths to steady her nerves, but it didn't seem to be working very well. Sipping on her water lightly, she wished Drew were here with her. He was good during emergencies, and this one topped the cake. She fought back the urge to burst into tears. She needed to pull herself together before the police arrived.

The police sirens in the distance grew louder as the responders neared the crime scene. Around the harbor, fishermen started to arrive and head towards their boats. Tourists were unpacking their cars and preparing for a fun day on the water. Little did they know that the most gruesome crime in

Plymouth's current history had been committed right here on the waterfront. The calm, beautiful summer day had just taken an ominous turn.

11

S HIFTING NERVOUSLY ON the hard wooden bench, Kat continued to scan the parking area, waiting for Plymouth Police and Fire to respond. She didn't have to wait long.

Several Plymouth Police cruisers, a firetruck, and two ambulances arrived at the parking lot closest to the water and screeched to a stop close to the pier. Various other unmarked vehicles arrived shortly behind them, and Kat saw someone dressed in a suit speaking with the group before they approached the crime scene. She felt her hands still shaking and drank some more water as the EMTs and uniformed police rushed past her towards *Dolphin II.* Suddenly, she realized that she recognized the "suit" who approached her with a genuinely concerned look on his face as someone she'd known since high school. Ian Miller, formerly a uniformed officer, apparently had become a homicide detective in Plymouth. Kat hadn't seen him since their last high school reunion and felt a brief wave of relief wash over her as she tried to smile at the friendly, familiar face.

"Kat...Oh my gosh...are you alright?" Ian reached out as he approached, gently touched Kat's arm, then glanced over at the boat. "I take it you found him?" Kat looked slightly queasy and shook her head in affirmation. Ian reached inside his suit coat pocket, pulled out a business card with his contact information on it, and handed it to Kat. "Okay, I'll need to talk to you, but we can do it later today. Please, go home and write down everything you can remember both when you arrived here and when you got on that boat and found the victim. I'll be at the station later this evening. You can stop by when it's convenient for you. Please, take it easy. And Kat? Please don't talk about this to anyone, at least until after we've gotten an official statement from you, ok?"

Kat readily agreed and stood up, a bit unsteadily at first, thanking Ian for letting her leave before gathering up her bags and heading towards the parking lot and her Jeep. Feeling extremely anxious and unnerved, she couldn't wait to get as far away from Plymouth Harbor as she possibly could. The image of Will Clarke with the harpoon sticking out of him, with his eyes wide open like a horror mask, made her feel nauseous all over again. She purposely picked up her pace and breathed a sigh of relief as she approached the back of her vehicle, quickly stuffing her gear away before turning around towards the driver's door, unlocking it, and jumping in, Kat noticed someone had stuck some sort of flyer or ad under her windshield wiper on the driver's side. "Oh, for crying out loud!" Kat snorted. "How annoying!"

With an irritated groan, she climbed back out of the Jeep and reached across the windshield to retrieve the flapping paper protruding from under the wiper blade. She grabbed it in her fist and crawled back inside the Jeep, tossing the paper on the passenger seat. Suddenly, she noticed something on the seat that wasn't there before. Lying on the passenger seat was a small, round button-like item. Picking it up, she realized it was a smooth piece of round scrimshaw. Adorned in black ink, she read the initials "B.W." on the back side. "Oh my God!" Kat had a sharp intake of breath. "What the...is this stolen scrimshaw?" Kat turned the piece over and over in her hand, carefully placing it in the cupholder of her center console. "Who put this in my vehicle?" she wondered as she turned the key in the ignition. Before backing out of the lot, Kat pus on her seatbelt and picked up the wrinkled paper to see what it was advertising. As she reads it, she instantly feels as if someone has punched her in the stomach and she can't catch her breath. Her hands begin to tremble. She slowly looked up and glanced uneasily around the parking lot. The scene down on the pier was in full swing, and a crowd was forming around the yellow crime scene tape the police put up. The parking lot looked slightly busier than it did earlier, and the arriving tourists, yet unaware of the murder scene on the waterfront, seemed to be going about their business as usual. Nothing looked out of place on this sunny summer day, except the now crumpled paper Kat held in her right hand. She could feel her eyes begin to sting with tears as she stared at the message, hastily scrawled in block letters across the page: MIND YOUR OWN BUSINESS!

12

KAT FELT LIKE the blood had been drained from her body. She froze, as her mind tried to comprehend the meaning of the note. For a few seconds, none of it made sense. Then, the gravity of the situation began to sink in.

"Whhhaaat the..." Kat mumbled out loud, reading the handwritten, single line over and over again. Someone had watched her board the boat and discover the body. Obviously, they knew she called the police. That same someone had to have been the person who left her the note. And the piece of scrimshaw. That someone was probably the person who impaled poor Will Clarke. That person also knew who *she* was.

Tossing the note onto the passenger seat once again, Kat leaned forward and rested her forehead on the steering wheel. Trying to hold back the tears welling up in her eyes, she breathed slowly and deliberately to regain some sense of calm so she could drive home. She could hear her own heartbeat pounding in her ears. Everything that she had experienced in the last half hour or so had totally overwhelmed her, and she knew she had to go to the Plymouth Police as soon as she was able. Ian Miller needed to know that she might be more involved in the murder now than she had originally intended and she needed reassurance that she would be protected. Her head was spinning. What if the killer thought Kat saw them actually go to the boat? How soon before her arrival had the homicide taken place? And that murder weapon?! What the hell!? Who has a whaling harpoon lying around? Kat was hopeful that the detectives would be able to answer some of the questions that started popping into her head quicker than she could think of her own answers.

"I don't know anything about the murder," Kat thought to herself. "I just arrived on the scene at the wrong time, but the killer might not know this and think I can identify them. Holy crap...

I could be in real danger until they catch who did this!"

It was then Kat realized that the person who committed the murder could also be the same person who broke into the whaling museum. That meant Capt. Will Clarke was most likely impaled by the stolen harpoon!

"Oh my God," Kat muttered to herself. "This is getting more confusing by the minute. Why would these two events be related? What the hell is going on? I need to get out of here. Now."

She slipped the Jeep into reverse, backed out of the parking space, and with a determined mindset, started her journey home. Shortly after leaving the parking lot, she passed a van headed toward the pier with the ominous affiliation painted on its side, *Plymouth County Medical Examiners' Office*. She shuddered nervously and continually checked her rearview mirror, gripping the steering wheel tighter by the mile. Kat didn't relax until she turned into her driveway twenty minutes later.

After hitting the button on the garage door opener and pulling inside the garage, Kat felt a sense of relief hearing the door slam down behind her. Sitting in the semi-dark garage, inside the Jeep beside the lawn mower, snow blower, and all her garden tools, felt safe. It took a minute to collect her thoughts before entering the house. She knew she had to get her wits about her and drive to the police station. But right now, she needed to go inside and unwind for a little bit.

Kat let Dash out to do his business. He'd been waiting patiently, and her arrival home signaled his best chance of getting outside again. She grabbed the note off the passenger seat with a tissue, not sure if the police would check for fingerprints, considering the new connection to the museum break-in, and got out before unlocking the door leading into the house. Entering her familiar kitchen instantly set Kat at ease. Everything looked normal and more importantly, *felt* normal. Dash hopped off his bed in the sun, gracefully stretching his muscular little legs behind him, and trotting over to greet her as she sets her stuff down on the granite counter. Kat bent down, scooped her little boy up in her arms, and snuggled with him for a moment while closing her eyes and wishing the day had been very different. She found a zip lock bag and inserted the note to bring to the police station later. In a separate bag, she put the piece of scrimshaw. All the happy things she was anticipating that morning had vanished the minute she'd walked up those steps on *Dolphin II* to find Will Clarke's lifeless body, stuck to the deck of the wheelhouse in a pool of his own blood. Not a good way to start the day.

13

AFTER UNPACKING CAMERA equipment and pulling up a stool to the kitchen counter, Kat quickly typed out a text on her phone and let Drew know that she needed to talk with him at some point, whether it be right away or later this afternoon. She decided against texting the gist of her day to him right now, as she knew it would only signal a huge alarm with him. So, she planned on spilling the whole story as soon as they could talk. Kat waited for a response and within a few minutes, her husband texted back saying that he is in the field at the moment, but would call her at 3 pm "her" time if that would be ok. He asked if it is an emergency, and she sent back a smiley face and a simple "no." The emoji didn't truly reflect her current sentiments, but she wanted to keep him at ease. She was glad he could call her back before she went to the Plymouth Police station later that evening, rather than after. She still felt nervous and knew Drew would help put her fears to rest when they could finally converse.

Kat dug up a lined notebook and flipped it open to a clean page. Staring off into space and tapping her pen absently on the counter, she replayed her arrival at the pier earlier that day and tried to remember what she saw. She jotted down the people she remembered seeing arrive near her in the lot, although nobody had parked next to her, and everybody seemed to be minding their own business for the most part. She admitted to herself that she was primarily focused on her upcoming interview and not really paying attention to the parking lot and its clientele when she originally arrived.

Before boarding the boat, Kat recalled seeing a long, white, partially open zippered bag lying on the pier with what looked like the gear for a windsurfer: a sail and lines rolled up inside. While walking past it, she had casually wondered where someone would be able to windsurf near the busy harbor area, but quickly dismissed the thought as she approached *Dolphin II*.

"I guess I'd better be sure and put that down," Kat mused to herself. She continued to focus on remembering the details of her arrival on the boat and the subsequent discovery of Will Clarke. She tried to write down as much as she could recall without appearing too dramatic, but the memory of the gruesome scene kept popping into her head as she tried to describe what she had witnessed. Not much had looked out of place or disheveled and Kat wrote that down as well.

Fifteen minutes later, she was satisfied with her written statement for the police and pushed it aside on the counter. She closed her eyes before putting her forehead down on the cool granite for a moment. She sensed movement beneath her stool and knew Dash would be willing to listen to her. He always was!

"This has been the worst freakin' day in a loooong time," Kat announced to Dash, who was sitting patiently beside her and staring up. "It didn't go at all as planned, and worse, the killer just might think that *I* saw something. Oh my God, Dash. I hope this crime is solved quickly. I might be in danger, and I'm not quite sure what to do. I can't wait to talk to Drew later. I wonder if Ian Miller has officially found a connection between the murder and the museum robbery."

Dash stared directly at Kat, then blinked twice, as if to affirm Kat's reason for alarm. He stayed close and waited. He knew what was coming next. He slowly stretched out his front legs and lay flat on the floor. He watched and waited some more. Kat got up and moved outside to her back deck, flopping down on a lounge chair in the sun. He followed and jumped up on the end and curled into a soft furry ball.

Kat closed her eyes and focused on the sounds around her. She tried to slow down her mind and calm her still jangled nerves. Listening to the birds chirping and talking back and forth across the yard and feeling the breezes blowing through the hemlock trees surrounding her was one of her methods that usually worked. Taking slow, deliberate breaths and thinking clearly about the events that had taken place already today, helped put an order to some of it as Kat tried to fit the pieces together into a somewhat less intimidating situation. She wanted to present the whole murder investigation to Drew as something he shouldn't really be worried about, even though she was feeling pretty anxious herself since finding the note on her windshield. She knew she couldn't intentionally leave that detail out of their upcoming conversation, but she also didn't want him to abandon his project and fly home to be with her and do what? Hopefully, her assurance that she would be meeting with Ian Miller later that night would help ease any concerns he might have after hearing the whole story.

In the meantime, Kat decided she would try to relax and attempt to connect with Mac, her second great-grandfather, who randomly appeared in her life last year and helped her solve a long-held family secret with unexpected financial gains and surprising spiritual support. Mac, (formally known as Quinn MacIntyre) was technically what most people would call a "ghost." (Although he preferred the term "spirit") Mac had become adept at the ability to manifest himself in various forms in order to communicate with Kat. Natural settings and direct desire on Kat's part often prefaced Mac's arrival. Kat had become familiar with the odd sensations that ran up and down her spine and the tingling in her hands signaling Mac's presence. She never knew exactly where or how he would show up, but the idea that he was within "responding range" wasn't nearly as surprising as it used to be. In fact, Kat had grown to feel rather comfortable in Mac's presence.

She wanted to communicate with Mac today and knew he wouldn't be far away. He rarely was. She could almost feel his presence already.

Focus. Breathe. She began to feel a slight tingle running down her arms, into her hands. She sensed he was somewhere nearby.

Showtime.

14

K AT FELT THE sun on her face as she closed her eyes and focused on contacting Mac through thought. She began a dialogue in her head that was unrehearsed and from her heart. She couldn't quite understand why she felt she needed Mac's presence to help process what she had witnessed earlier today. The tingling sensation spiraling down her spine continued to manifest, and she could feel her hands nearly vibrating. From past experiences, Kat knew what this physical sensation meant.

Dash remained quietly lying at the end of the cushion, staring out towards the backyard that melted into the woods behind Kat's house. Huge white pine trees and hemlocks created a ring around the perimeter of the yard. Aside from the bird conversations echoing back and forth across the property, the slight breeze through the trees was all Kat could hear until Dash made a small noise interrupting her attempt at contacting Mac.

She opened her eyes and looked down from her deck in the direction Dash continued to stare. There she saw a large, beautiful white-tailed deer standing at the edge of her yard and staring up in their direction. Standing perfectly still and curiously twitching its white tail, the deer appeared to look directly at Kat. Dash barely moved a muscle as Kat stared back at the calm, majestic animal. She felt herself holding her breath. She could feel him.

And then she heard him.

"Hello, Kat. Yes, it's me, Mac. I'm happy to hear from you and thank you for thinking of me!"

"H-h-hello Mac. Wow…I wasn't exactly sure what form you might take or if you could even manifest here today. This is quite the surprise! Thank you for allowing me to contact you, and I hope I'm not, uh, bothering you?" Kat still wasn't sure what Mac *did* while residing on the other side. She knew he was an artist, but he seemed readily available the few times she had intentionally contacted him. And, he had acted genuinely pleased to interact with her each time. It was almost as if he was waiting for her to reach out. Like he *knew* when she needed to talk with him.

"I sensed you trying to get in touch with me through your meditation, and I am aware of the horrible situation you found yourself in this morning at the pier. I was hoping you might request my assistance, and I am anxious to help you. I'm sorry for your fear and shock today."

Kat exhaled slowly, then took a deep breath before continuing. She could feel tears welling up inside her and became frustrated with her own lack of self-control. She sat up straighter and looked down at the deer in her yard like a trusted friend. It remained motionless yet stared intently at her. Not feeling at all self-conscious, the story of finding Will Clarke's body and then the note on her windshield tumbled out of her before she could stop herself. The entire time, the deer continued to stand stoically and appeared to listen. Mentally running through the morning's drama once again, Kat fought back tears a few times while recounting the saga but eventually managed to spill out her story and felt immediately better after having done so. She blew her nose, pulled herself together, and then continued her conversation with Mac.

"I'm so sorry…this whole situation has been incredibly unnerving, and I can't believe I found poor Will Clarke murdered in such a violent and bizarre way on his own boat. There's got to be something we can do! I'm meeting with the police later, and I don't know much, only what I saw. But, it's too weird; the robbery at the whaling museum just happened, and now this!! That stolen harpoon *has* to be the murder weapon, but why? None of it makes any sense."

"I agree. None of this makes any sense…right now. But your safety is of utmost importance, and somebody near you thinks you either know or saw something relating to the murder. There's a reason somebody stole and then used that particular weapon. It's meaningful. You must protect yourself in whatever manner best

suits you. In the meantime, I will be starting my investigation on this side. As your "remote location" contact, we can work together. As I previously mentioned, we both have scenarios that we must participate in on our respective sides in order to progress within our personal growth plans. I will be gathering pertinent information on my side to be of help on your side, and together we will solve this murder. All while allowing the police to believe they have succeeded solely by their own clever devices!"

Kat laughed out loud at Mac's humorous nod towards the "mortal man's ego" they both knew existed within law enforcement agencies when handling a case. Regardless of the help or advancement Kat or Mac could potentially provide, they both knew the police would claim sole credit for solving any murder mysteries. Oh well! It was expected and assumed that it went with the territory and the police would discount information provided from any "alternative sources," especially any that might be considered "ghostly!"

"Ok. In the meantime, I have to meet with the Plymouth Police later today and I will know more after that meeting. If you can start doing whatever you do on your side, maybe we can get together again in a few days and compare notes. I think if you can start looking into the ancestors who have passed on from Will Clarke's family, maybe we can find a clue that links past to present, something...anything."

"I agree. I will begin my investigation right away. I feel there must be another link between the killer and Will Clarke as well. In the meantime, please be mindful of who is around you and I will remain close by. I do not want any harm to find you as we work together. Pay close attention when you feel my attempt to contact you, as I will let you know if I sense you are in any sort of imminent danger. We shall reconvene soon. Please remain aware. Oh...and Kat, I'm happy to be working in conjunction with you again. I do believe we strike a good balance together."

Kat remained seated, quietly watching the deer who remained standing near the edge of her backyard. He slowly turned his head as if to gaze into the deep woods behind him. Glancing back once quickly in her direction, he dipped his head as if to nod, then flicked his impressive white tail rapidly. Mac instantly disappeared into the thicket of green behind him with one graceful leap and left Kat staring at an empty yard.

15

KAT REMAINED SITTING on her deck with Dash still close by, taking everything in. She felt better after having the conversation with Mac, but she was still very concerned about the letter on her windshield and who might have thought she had witnessed Will's murder. For the hundredth time since arriving home, Kat racked her brain for a clue as to *who* might have the motive to commit the murder and *what* that motive might be. She knew Ian Miller wouldn't share any vital information with her, but any piece of the puzzle that he might be able to offer could potentially help her and Mac in the long run. She knew, instantly, that this was another one of those times when she and Mac might "work" together and solve a mystery. Their collaborations prior to this were very productive, and they discovered that they each brought a different set of "skills" to the table, but ultimately found the answers they were seeking by combining their efforts.

She was looking forward to meeting with Ian and filling him in on the letter she found on her windshield. Somehow, preparing to share it all with the police seemed to make her feel better in that moment, although the big question as to who else was involved still loomed large.

After a few quiet minutes of reflection, Kat got up from her lounge chair and Dash instantly hopped off too. She went inside to put his harness on and grab a leash after deciding they would take a ride to the beach so she could get out and walk for a bit. She had time before she would be talking to Drew and then going to the police station about this whole mess, and a walk on the beach always made her feel better.

"C'mon, boy, let's go! We'll take a little walk on the beach before we have to recount this whole story a few more times. Ugh! Hard to believe this much crap could happen before noontime!" Kat snapped the leash onto Dash, and they hopped into her Jeep and headed towards the beach. Knowing what was ahead of her this afternoon sent a shiver down Kat's spine. But she felt better knowing she had Mac on her team, whatever that might mean. She still wasn't sure how they might unravel this murder mystery, but now that she was involved, she realized she needed all the help she could get.

Kat enjoyed her walk with Dash on the beach, and when they came home, she had lunch and caught up with her cousin Lucy from Martha's Vineyard on the phone. Without revealing the details that she would be sharing with the police, Kat explained that she could discuss them more after her meeting with Ian Miller. While they were chatting, Kat got interrupted and her phone beeped several times indicating an incoming call.

"I have to go, Lucy! It's the Plymouth Police calling, and I have to take the call. I'll absolutely call you after I know more and can fill you in." With that, Kat clicked over to the incoming call and was greeted by Ian Miller who sounded tired and rushed, but friendly, nonetheless.

"Hi Kat, sorry to bother you. I know we were going to meet later today, but I'd like to reschedule our meeting until Monday. I've got a lot going on today and I'm anxious to get your statement. I do, however, have one quick question for you before we meet on Monday."

"Of course, I totally understand. I'll be available all-day Monday and can come down to the station whenever it's convenient for you. Please ask your question then I have one more bit of information to tell you about that happened after I saw you at the murder scene earlier today."

"Okay, great. I'm just wondering if you happened to see a white canvas and nylon-type athletic bag on or near the pier when you arrived on this morning. It would have been approximately six to seven feet long with a zipper on it. Like a large gear bag."

Kat immediately remembered seeing a bag loosely matching that description lying on the pier when she arrived to meet Will Clarke. In fact, she had walked right by it. She had included it in her statement that she had written immediately after she had arrived home, as Ian had suggested.

"Yes!!" exclaimed Kat. I did see a large, white nylon or canvas bag with a zipper lying on the pier, not far from the bench I had been sitting on while I waited for you to arrive. It was there when I arrived to meet Will Clarke, and it was there when I left after your arrival. The other thing I wanted to mention to you was what I found when I got back to my vehicle after the responders all arrived and I went to leave. I found a handwritten note under the windshield wiper on my Jeep. It said, 'MIND YOUR OWN BUSINESS.' I also found a round piece of scrimshaw on the seat of my Jeep. It has initials on one side and an image on the other, etched in black ink. I think it's one of the stolen pieces."

A palpable silence from Ian's end of the phone line raised Kat's fear level a notch. She knew Ian instantly understood someone had apparently connected Kat to the murder scene, and it was most probable that she could now be in danger. Although she truly had no knowledge of the killer, her arrival after the murder had spooked the killer, and they were at least aware of Kat's involvement. And they had to have been close by when she went back to her Jeep.

"I'll check with the town to find out if the parking lot cameras were working down by the pier and if we can get hold of the footage from today. We might get lucky and see who dropped the bag and/or who might have been hanging around when you were leaving. Please bring the note with you on Monday. We'll check it for prints and in the meantime, we're checking the bag for prints and its contents for a possible owner. It looks as if it's a gear bag for a windsurfer; the stuff inside fits that description, but we're guessing in this case it was used to transport the murder weapon. And Kat, I'm very concerned about the note you found on your windshield. I'm going to have a cruiser parked down the street from the end of your driveway 24/7 until we have more information. Please be careful, don't talk about this case to anyone, and please remember to bring the note with you on Monday."

They set up a time to meet on Monday and hung up. Kat felt a shiver and was glad she had the opportunity to tell Ian about the note, even if she wasn't going to the police station today. She would just have to downplay any dangerous-sounding information when she talks with Drew later and unfortunately, would have to mention the police detail Ian set up near their house. She knew *that* wouldn't go over well, and Drew might just decide to come home early. Now, she was beginning to think that that might not be the worst idea.

Later that afternoon, Kat was curled up in the most comfortable hammock, trying to read and find a distraction from the whirl of activity. When the phone rang, her heart skipped a beat when she saw it was Drew. He seemed anxious to chat. She mustered her bravest voice and answered quickly.

"Hey...how's it going? It's pouring rain here, so we're holed up in our hotel waiting for a break. I miss you guys!" Drew was helping an archeological team on a dig located in Canada and wasn't expected home for another two weeks. Kat had become accustomed to having time alone when he was traveling for work and usually enjoyed those breaks, but the latest turn of events had shaken her more than she wanted to admit to herself. She tried to sound confident and upbeat when she answered, but the bravado wavered a bit in her voice and Drew picked up on it instantly. He sensed something was off, but knew Kat would be unable to contain any emotional reactions for very long, so he was prepared for whatever spilled out.

"Hi!! We're great, right, Dash?!" She looked down at Dash who seemed to stare back with an almost skeptical look. "And we miss you too! Sorry to hear about all the rain. Will it affect your departure date?"

"No, it shouldn't," Drew responded. "I worked a few extra days when the crew took off over the holiday, so I'm ahead of schedule. So, what's going on?"

"Well...uh... well, we sort of had a major event happen today and unfortunately, I became part of it...but I'm FINE! You don't have to worry..." Kat's voice trailed off briefly, but she rallied on and continued trying to convince Drew all was well before she finally told him about stumbling upon the murder victim.

Drew chuckled, unaware of the upcoming revelation and description of the situation Kat had encountered. "Maybe you'd better just tell me what happened!"

Kat took a deep breath and began her tale of horror. She started with her job offer from the Chamber of Commerce and setting up the whale watching trip with Captain Will, then finally eased into the ghastly part about the murder and, unfortunately, finding the victim in the wheelhouse along with the potentially stolen whaling harpoon.

Drew was shocked and of course instantly concerned when she got to the part about finding the note on her windshield. When she described finding the scrimshaw piece on her seat, he was momentarily at a loss for words. He listened carefully while she explained seeing Ian Miller on the scene and how she set up a time to meet with him on Monday. She tried her best to sound brave and cover up the nervousness she was feeling, but he knew she was only trying to convince him so he wouldn't worry. Of course, he wanted to book a flight home the following day, but Kat managed to put his mind at ease when she revealed that Ian had set up a surveillance team near the end of their driveway, watching her 24/7, and she felt relatively safe having them nearby.

By the end of their lengthy conversation, Kat had convinced Drew to remain on location and promised to keep him in the loop daily as to what was happening with the case. She knew her meeting with Ian would be important, but she also made sure to let Drew know that she had contacted Mac, and he was beginning his own research on the "other side." He understood the "time passage" that had been previously opened between Kat and Mac was a special bond, and Mac had only positive and helpful intent when he worked in conjunction with Kat. They were an unusual and effective duo. Drew was relieved that Mac had been called in to keep tabs on Kat. It never hurts to have an "eye in the sky" on your team.

By the time they hung up, Kat felt relieved having shared all the information with Drew and that he agreed to let the Plymouth Police handle the situation for the time being. The fact that the police were keeping an eye on the house and Kat offered some relief, though Drew hoped the case would be solved quickly and Kat would no longer be involved on any level.

Kat just wanted to get through the meeting with the Plymouth Police on Monday and hoped they would determine who the killer was quickly and without any more incidents. In the back of her mind, she knew Mac would uncover any clues that might link the past to the present, but for now, she would just keep a low profile and let the police do their thing while she and Mac did theirs.

~ 47 ~

16

PATRICK WALSH WAS hosing down the hull of *Velella* Saturday afternoon when his phone rang. Feeling annoyed, he shut off and then threw down the hose, rummaged in his pocket, and yanked out his phone. His annoyance quickly turned to surprise when he saw Plymouth Police flash up on his phone, indicating the identity of the incoming call. Clearing his throat first, Patrick answered the call, trying to sound casual, but any calls from the Plymouth Police weren't usually good news in his past dealings with them.

Patrick listened suspiciously while a homicide detective, Ian Miller, explained the reason for the call. He stood silently while the detective briefly detailed Will Clarke's murder at the town pier. After some generic questions, Detective Miller asked Patrick if he could arrange to come down to the police station on Monday, as they had some questions they wanted to run by him. Shocked and caught off guard by the call, Patrick readily agreed to go to the station on Monday and took Ian Miller's cell phone number. When he hung up, his hands were shaking, and the familiar feeling of dread returned from the mere thought of meeting with the detective. Why did they want to talk to him? He couldn't stand that guy Clarke and yes, he'd beat the crap out of him a few times, but he'd had it coming. Not a loss as far as he was concerned. He'd always hated cops and to be honest, he told himself that he really didn't feel too bad about that moron Will Clarke either; he'd gotten what he deserved. No big deal. He'd be hard pressed to mourn that guy's murder when he talked to the cops. Now, there was one less whale boat to deal with this summer, and it was as simple as that.

He went back to washing his boat and started thinking about seeing the police on Monday.

This whole thing didn't feel good, and now he was starting to worry. It might look like he had a motive if they asked around. Hell, he could probably find a motive for knocking off just about anybody in this stupid town if they pissed him off enough. He was just trying to get ahead. Why couldn't they just leave him the bloody hell alone?

17

JONATHAN WOODWORTH GROANED and rolled over, reaching blindly to shut the blaring alarm off coming from his phone on the nightstand. His head was pounding, and he felt a wave of bile rise in his throat when he sat upright. He threw back the sheet, dashed into his bathroom, and wretched several times. Taking a damp facecloth, he scrubbed his face, staring at himself in the mirror. He had to admit it; he looked like hell. Messy, greasy hair stood upright, bags sat under his weary eyes, and the once glowing summer tan now looked sallow in the fluorescent light of his bathroom. Jon ran his hands through his hair and leaned closer to the mirror. Squinting at himself closely, he figured he could get himself cleaned up to make it to his hearing with plenty of time to spare.

He had stayed out late the two previous nights and drank way too many beers. It briefly helped him avoid thinking about what he would have to do if he was found guilty of any charges. But, the worst part was that he couldn't recall big chunks of time that had occurred over the weekend. He tried to remember getting home the evening before and all he could draw was a blank. Racking his brain to recall the previous forty-eight hours was useless. Apparently, he'd had more beers than he remembered. Well, it doesn't matter. He'd already invested a ton of money in his new boat and whale watch business, and there was no way he would just step back and let someone else, *anyone* else, reap the reward that he was entitled to. He'd never been that pushover kind of guy.

He'd handle it using *his* own style. One way or another.

Jon took a quick look through his closet, threw some khaki pants and a button-down shirt on the bed to wear to the hearing, and hopped into the shower. While the hot water rolled down his back, he closed his eyes and once again tried, in vain, to recall any of the details of the last few days, but he felt as if his head was full of cobwebs. Toweling off and dressing, he began to seriously worry about the upcoming hearing with NOAA and felt his anger rising with every thought. He couldn't stop thinking about who could have ratted him out. An ex-employee? A pissed off relative? A competitor? He wouldn't put it past those other a-holes who ran the whale watch boats. Hell, it could even be an old girlfriend with an axe to grind. He knew there were enough of them floating around out there. Grinning to himself despite the gravity of the situation, he felt somewhat proud of the fact that he'd stepped on more than a few toes along the way. Hey, that's how he got where he was. He always came out on top. Today would be no different. Screw them all.

18

MONDAY MORNING STARTED dark and windy with whitecaps slipping across Plymouth Harbor. The northeast wind bit through the black, hooded sweatshirt and threadbare tee shirt while the scrawny, young man yanked up his hood and glanced furtively around the mostly deserted town pier. There were remnants of the yellow crime scene tape flapping around the posts on the pier near where *Dolphin II* had been docked. Brian Buckley flicked his cigarette into the water and sat down on the bench attached to the main dock. Random gusts whipped his hair across his face, and the spray of rain spittle stung when he turned into the wind. He looked around, saw nobody on the piers, and stared again at the space *Dolphin II* had previously occupied. All was quiet here today. The whale watch boat had been towed away. The empty slip was a far cry from the mayhem that had taken place on Saturday morning. He'd disappeared as soon as the cops arrived. He'd seen that woman with the camera stuff board the boat, then later head to her Jeep. He knew she must have been the one to find that dead guy.

When he arrived Saturday morning, Brian was one of the few early birds in the parking lot. The sun was just beginning to come up, and the harbor was quiet without much boat activity happening that early. He'd heard that a few local scallopers were looking for day workers, and he thought he'd come down and see if he could go out for the day and make some scratch. Things had been tough lately, and he'd been looking for work here and there. He parked at the far end of the lot and got out of his car. When he got to the pier, he realized that he'd missed the scallop boat he'd hoped to work on that day and lost out on joining the crew. He'd been pissed off and sat down at the picnic table located off the far side of the parking lot. Now nearly hidden by tall weeds and damp, marshy grass, he flopped down at the grimy, carved-up wooden picnic table to plan his next move. Not caring that it wasn't quite 6:00 am, he carefully slipped out a half-smoked blunt from his cigarette pack and lit it up. After taking a few long hits and feeling his mood lighten, Brian spotted someone walking down the pier very quickly. It was hard to see that morning because it was just barely getting light;, but the person looked like they had a large, white bag they were carrying toward the docked boats. He continued to casually smoke his weed and watched while the figure stopped momentarily near *Dolphin II*.

After a brief pause, he hoisted the bag with some difficulty, threw it onto the deck of the whale watch boat, and climbed aboard over the railings, as there was no ramp. The person disappeared as Brian continued to sit and watch from his secluded table and continued pondering his options.

Within about ten minutes, Brian watched through lazy eyes while some-one else appeared on the pier, also headed toward *Dolphin II*. They had been carrying a small cooler, a black canvas duffle bag with long handles, and a small toolbox. Brian watched them hoist their gear up onto the deck of the boat, then climb aboard much like the first person had. He then disappeared for a few moments and reappeared rolling a portable ramp which he pro-ceeded to set up between the boat and the dock. This person clearly knew his way around the boat, and Brian assumed it was the owner, Capt. Will, whom he had read about in the paper. He then disappeared out of Brian's view, and he never saw him again.

Just about the time Brian had decided to go get a cup of coffee and start-ed to get up from the picnic table, he spotted the first figure he had seen board the vessel running quickly down the ramp of *Dolphin II*, carrying the long, white bag he had thrown onto the deck of the boat before climbing aboard. Brian stood quietly behind the tall grass and cat-o'-nine tails sur-rounding the neglected picnic area, watching. The person who had been on the boat was now leaving quickly. He was clearly a man, and he deliberately threw down the white bag he had been carrying when he originally arrived on the pier. Leaving it behind, he picked up his pace and disappeared around the corner into the parking lot. Brian could see him approaching the area where he later learned Kat's Jeep had been parked.

Getting up from the table, Brian backtracked towards his own car, noticed nothing was amiss in the parking lot, and decided to go get coffee. Before reaching his own car, he wandered over near some trash barrels at the edge of the parking lot. Something small and round caught his eye, lying among old wrappers, sand, and small stones on the worn, cracked pavement. He picked it up, looked at it briefly, then stuffed it in his pocket. Moving on, he killed some time at the donut shop and decided he'd return to the pier, hoping to get lucky and find a fishing crew that needed some day help.

Shortly before 8 am, he returned to the pier and was headed towards the fishing boats when he saw a woman heading down the pier who appeared to be approaching *Dolphin II*. She was carrying photography equipment and went up the ramp that had been set up, disappearing from view for a minute or two before coming back out with all her gear and sitting down on the deck of the whale tour boat. Within a short time, Brian heard police sirens and saw ambulances heading their way. He watched as the Plymouth Police arrived with all the emergency vehicles. Then, he could see the woman with the camera talking with police before she returned to her Jeep. Brian had observed all this from the sidelines, unnoticed. He'd also seen the person who approached the area near the woman's Jeep before she returned to it. At this point, he figured he had no reason to get involved and had no plan whatsoever to talk with the police. The last thing he needed was to be a witness either *for* or *against* somebody.

Brian spent the last two days thinking about what he had seen on Saturday at the Pier. Now it was Monday, and he was beginning to wonder if maybe he *should* talk to the Plymouth Police. He heard about the murder on TV, although they didn't seem to have many details to reveal. He decided he would go back down to the town pier and take a look around again. Now he was back, and it's feeling was creepy. Will Clarke's tour boat was gone from its berth, and he guessed the police were still looking for his killer. He thought that he just might know more than he wanted to know about who killed Will Clarke. He saw three people boarding that boat on Saturday, and only two walked off. The other was carried off in the body bag.

And then there's that piece of scrimshaw. He picked it up in the parking lot on Saturday. He'd almost forgotten about it until he reached into his jeans pocket and found it among his change. Looking more closely at it, the images seemed to depict some sort of whaling scene on both sides. It had delicate, black ink etching and was worn satiny smooth, studying it as he turned it over and over between his fingers. Brian wondered who had dropped it? It might not mean anything, but he remembered hearing something about stolen pieces of scrimshaw when the whaling museum in Plymouth had been broken into on Memorial Day Weekend. Maybe this piece was worth something. Was this part of the stolen property? Maybe there was a reward, and maybe the person who broke into the museum is the same person who dropped this in the parking lot! Maybe he *should* go to the police.

19

ON MONDAY MORNING, Kat collected her notebook and sat on the couch next to Dash before preparing to leave for her appointment at the police station. Stroking his soft, warm head, he closed his eyes contentedly and snuggled deeper into his blanket on the end of the couch.

"Well, little guy, I'll be back at some point, but I'm not sure when." Dash partially opened one amber colored eye and looked sleepily up at Kat. "I really have nothing to offer Ian as far as information goes. I can't understand what all this has to do with me. I definitely can't tell him I have a "secret source" helping me try and solve this murder, and that he lives on the *other side*!! It would probably send my credibility down the hopper really quickly!"

Sitting very still and closing her eyes, Kat concentrated very deliberately on sending a quick mental "memo" to Mac. She wanted to let him know she was headed to see the police, and she would definitely "reach out" to him after she had gotten home. Not really being sure how this whole process of communicating with Mac actually worked, Kat took three deep breaths and stood up, ready to face the Plymouth Police.

When arriving at the police station, Kat became burdened by a little bit of apprehension. She had to admit it to herself. She knew she would have to recount much of her statement verbally to the police, in addition to her written account she had previously provided. Reliving the horrific scene again, even briefly, was still upsetting and not something she wished to continue to have to do. Hoping this will be her last visit here, Kat entered the lobby and waited quietly on the hard, metal chairs for Detective Ian Miller to escort her into his cramped, windowless office.

Suddenly, the glass door separating the waiting area from the back offices flew open and a large, rather grubby looking young man with greasy hair tied back in a ponytail and a Red Sox cap on backwards burst into the waiting area, muttering loudly and using swearwords one after the other. Taking three long strides, he reached the outside door. He never looked in Kat's direction, but she could sense a black rage in his eyes. He pushed the door outward with his splayed hands and kicked the bottom of it with his heavy work boots at the same time before blasting out into the parking lot. The last she saw of him, he was turning the corner and heading out of sight, his hands swinging in fists at his sides. Somebody was looking none too happy about his visit here.

Within thirty seconds, Kat saw Ian coming through the same glass door the angry young man had just burst through. He had a tired look on his face. He smiled, greeting Kat in a friendly way, and she felt instantly more relaxed about being there. Escorting her into his office stacked with files and more files, he motioned to the chair across from his desk and turned to shut his door before sitting down too.

"Thanks so much for coming down, Kat. I really appreciate it. I know we haven't seen each other in a few years, but regardless of the situation, I'm happy to see you and wish it were under different circumstances. Now, give me a minute to read your statement and we can go through it line by line. If you have anything else to add or remember any tiny detail along the way, tell me, and I can add it to your final statement. Even something that might not seem pertinent could be an important clue. I also need the letter you found on your windshield. Let's get started."

Nearly two hours later, Kat and Ian finished their meeting. By its conclusion, Kat felt comfortable around Ian and tried her best to remember every detail she could in order to help. She didn't feel as though she had much to offer, but he seemed grateful for everything that she had told him. Kat readily handed over the piece of scrimshaw she had found. Ian gingerly took it and compared it with pictures the museum had supplied of the stolen pieces. Although he didn't make any verbal confirmation, she could tell by his face that there was a match. He then examined the letter Kat had carefully put into a Ziplock and told her they would be trying to match prints with the crime scene and the murder weapon. He hinted that the murder suspect could possibly be the same person who broke into the museum, but he was waiting for positive identification from the museum curator that the murder weapon was indeed the one stolen over the long weekend. They were also in the process of getting video footage from the Town of Plymouth for the cameras located at the town pier. The museum would provide their video images from the break-in and robbery. Ian seemed confident that he could tie the events together, but he wasn't positive at this point about where that connection would take them. He put some of Kat's remaining fears to rest when he told her they would be continuing the surveillance on her house for the time being, and he would keep her in the loop with as much information as he could without compromising the case.

Kat was relieved to hear this information and knew Drew would be even happier to hear it as well. Before leaving Ian's office, Kat couldn't help but ask him about the angry man who had rushed out of the police station while she waited for her appointment.

Ian paused briefly, as if trying to decide whether to share this info with Kat or not. Before he could answer, Kat felt as if she needed to qualify her question as he seemed slightly uncomfortable answering.

"I'm only asking because I know I've seen him before, but I can't quite place it. He looks familiar, and he sure as hell looked pretty ticked off when he bolted out of here," Kat said innocently. Ian looked relieved and bent closer to Kat while he looked around to see if anyone was listening and said very quietly, "That was Mr. Patrick Walsh. He runs another tour boat company. The long, white duffle bag you saw lying on the pier when you arrived had some windsurfing gear inside, was probably used to transport the murder weapon, and had Mr. Walsh's name written on the inside of it. He claimed it had been stolen, and he didn't even know it was missing until we escorted him out to his pickup truck, where he said he had last stored it When we lifted the canvas top, big surprise! The bag was gone. Obviously, we're having prints pulled from it and when we put that info together with the museum and pier videos, we can start to form some sort of picture as to what went down on Saturday. And who might be involved."

Kat took this information and thanked Ian again for making her feel as safe as he could and left the police station. She had a lot to think about and couldn't wait to pass on what she'd learned to Mac.

TRAFFIC WAS LIGHT heading into Boston on Monday morning, which was a good thing because Jonathan Woodworth was already in a foul mood due to the situation he had to deal with, not to mention the giant headache that had developed once he had woken up and started driving. He'd mostly given up trying to figure out who had blown the whistle on him and reminded himself that he had already begun to even the score and would continue to do so. No point in looking back.

Staring angrily at the highway ahead, Jon told himself this hearing was a waste of his time, and somebody would pay big time when he was done with all this crap. He knew how to play dirty, and this time would be no different. He always got what he wanted.

Sitting in the hallway outside the NOAA offices in Boston, Jon absently tapped his left foot a bit too rapidly. A nervous tic had begun to play with the corner of his right eye, and he could feel it twitching, wondering if it was visible. Hoping it wasn't. He knew he had to keep his crap together during this meeting and falling apart today, especially after all he'd already accomplished, would screw things up royally.

"Suck it up, dude. Don't let 'em see ya sweat." Jon was finally summoned into the hearing room, and the thick, wooden door closed behind him with a dull thud.

****

Two hours later, Jonathan Woodworth slipped out of the hearing room and waited in the lobby for the elevator to take him back down to street level. Keeping his eyes down, he stepped in. Nobody else was inside, and after the door closed behind him, he banged his fists against the walls, vibrating the entire enclosure while it moved downward, and released the pent-up hurricane that had been brewing inside him. The elevator stopped on the first floor, and the three-second delay before the door opened allowed Jon to instantly shift back into the handsome, composed, professional-looking millennial he needed to be seen as. Purposefully, he stepped out into the hallway and strode out of the building towards his Range Rover.

21

KAT LEFT THE police station and headed home. Her head spun when she thought about the information she had learned on her short visit with Ian. She was comforted to know the police were actively working on the case, and she felt confident that eventually someone's fingerprints would appear in more than one place. She was shocked to learn that the mysterious bag on the pier belonged to someone named Patrick Walsh. She hadn't heard his name before, but she was sure she had seen his face somewhere prior to all of this happening. Kat absently flipped on the radio and turned it louder to hear the local news broadcast, which was updating information surrounding the whaling museum break-in and the murder weapon. Listening carefully, Kat learned that the museum officials had positively identified the harpoon used to murder Will Clarke. It had indeed been the same harpoon stolen during the robbery. They also mentioned that another item from the museum theft had been potentially found near the crime scene, but they were still in the process of making a positive identification of the item before releasing more information. Kat knew the scrimshaw piece she discovered inside her Jeep had to be part of the museum robbery, but the police weren't mentioning it yet.

"Hmmm..." mused Kat. "It sounded as if the police were gradually making a connection between the robbery and the murder. But why would the killer go through all the trouble to break into the museum, then commit a murder with a stolen artifact when he could have just boarded Will Clarke's boat, then shot or stabbed him? It sure would have been quicker and a hell of a lot easier." It seemed obvious to Kat that if the robbery suspect was determined, then they'd probably learn the identity of the murderer as well. But the problem was, who had the motive? Kat doubted she knew any of the potential suspects personally. Ian alluded to the fact that Patrick Walsh would certainly be of interest since he owned the bag transporting the murder weapon. If only Kat could find out more "inside" information. She knew Ian was limited with what he could share, but if she could somehow connect some more dots, maybe something would make more sense to her.

Nearing her driveway, she was relieved to see the unmarked police car parked in a shady spot off the main road, apparently keeping an eye on her property. Kat gave quick wave and continued up her driveway toward her house. Dash will be happy to see her, and she starts mentally planning the rest of her day. Kat decided that her "to-do" list would include some time to attempt a connection with Mac. She wants to compare "notes" and see if he has gleaned any info that might be helpful in untangling this mystery.

She laughed at the thought that only a year ago she had no idea who Quinn MacIntyre was, and since the "time passage" between them had been opened, they had become allies of a sort. They were related through bloodlines of course, but Kat knew they had a special bond that no one else in her immediate family could match. They had developed a method of communication that was difficult to explain to most people, but Kat loved it. Mac was her secret guide.

For now, Mac would remain a secret except with Drew and Dash (and to a certain degree, Kat's cousin Lucy who lives in Chilmark, on Martha's Vineyard).

Kat didn't know it yet, but Dash had opened his own "time passage" with Mac and was now an integral part of his team. Mac had some interesting information about Dash's past that he planned on sharing with Kat at some point, but it wouldn't be today.

Mac knew that when combined, they formed a triad of powerful energy. Remaining unseen, yet seeing it all, he couldn't help but smile too. It was all falling into place.

Kat arrived home, let Dash out to do his business, and sat down on her reclining chair to ponder her next move. Grabbing a pad of paper and a pen, she outlined the facts of the case as she knew them thus far. Frowning, she tapped her pen, trying to form links between the names on her list and how they might relate to one another. Something was missing. There had to be more information that would help.

Planning her call to Drew later that evening, Kat also decided that she would attempt to contact Mac and see how he was coming along on "his side." She felt as if she were wasting time for some reason and ought to be doing something more proactive. Grabbing the local newspaper, she thumbed through it until she came to the obituary section. She searched through the alphabetical list until she located the one she was looking for.

"William (Will) Clarke. 29 years old. Died in Plymouth last week under mysterious circumstances. Police are investigating the incident, which could possibly be linked to a stolen artifact from the whaling museum."

Family, short bio, visiting hours, and burial details were listed, and Kat decided in that instant that she would attend the funeral. She wouldn't go to the church, but she could hang around the cemetery and see who might attend his services. She knew that police often employed this sort of investigative technique to surveil friends, family, and potential suspects. The person being sought was often right in front of the very people looking for them. Kat figured it can't hurt to show up and stay in the background, as it might just turn up a useful clue. The burial would take place in two days, and she would be attending secretly.

Debating whether to mention this small detail to Drew, Kat finally decides that she will leave that information out during their upcoming conversation. There was no point in worrying Drew unnecessarily; the update from Ian confirming they were actively working on the case would hopefully quell most of his fears about her being involved. "Well," she figured. "I am already involved, so what is the harm in doing a little sleuthing?"

22

BRIAN BUCKLEY SAT alone at the bar inside the Depot. It was early afternoon, and only a few stragglers from lunch were still lingering nearby. A guy dressed in work boots with sleeves cut off his stained tee shirt sat at a high-top, flipping through his phone and nursing a beer. Meanwhile, an older couple sat at the bar a few seats away, staring at the Keno screen above the cash register. Brian had scored a few bucks from a poker game he played the night before, and decided he would go out and get himself a decent lunch. He ordered a twenty-ounce Bud and two burgers with fries. Sipping his beer, he glanced around the dimly lit bar, still occupied by his phone. He'd been questioning himself as to whether he should go talk to the Plymouth Police or not. He figured that the information he could tell them probably wasn't very important in the big scheme of things. He was going back and forth in his head while he waited for his burger when he glanced up at the TV above the bar and saw the local news flashing a segment about the recent murder in Plymouth Harbor.

The Chief of Police came on the screen, but Brian couldn't really hear him with the low volume. The captions said they were actively trying to match fingerprints from the crime scene to the earlier break-in at the whaling museum to connect the two crimes. It ended with another caption that said the case was ongoing and the Plymouth Police would appreciate any information the public could supply to help them solve these two crimes.

By the time the burgers arrived, Brian had made up his mind. He decided he would go to the Plymouth Police Department and tell them what he saw early Saturday morning. But first, he intended to eat his lunch, maybe go home and adjust his attitude, take a leisurely nap, and *then* think about when he might have some free time to go visit the police.

Brian reached into his pocket and felt the smooth-edged scrimshaw piece among some loose coins. He wondered if maybe he ought to turn it over to the cops when he went to the police station. He kind of hated to give it up, but figured if it's one of the stolen pieces, it might make him look good if he turned it in. Maybe. But what was the rush?

23

JONATHAN WOODWORTH SAT on his condo's back deck overlooking the 15th fairway at the elite Duxbury Country Club. The sun was starting to go down, and chugging back a beer, he lay flat on the lounge chair and closed his eyes. The headaches had returned, and he massaged his temples for a moment.

"Damn. It's gone from bad to worse." He'd replay the hearing he had in Boston over and over in his head, and it didn't go well. After all was said and done, he was slapped with a hefty fine and his license to conduct whale watching tours was revoked for seven consecutive days.

"Seven frickin' days and I can't do a damn charter...It's not fair...all I did was get a *little* too close to the damn whale and some goody two shoes had to send pictures in? Like, really?"

Jon was disgusted and vowed to continue to even the score as he finished his beer. Tossing the empty can in the trash, he went back inside and flipped open his laptop. Settling in his pricey leather recliner, he popped open another beer, took a long gulp, scrolling around until he found what he was looking for.

"Bingo. Here we go...obituaries...hmmmm...oh yeah...William Clarke," Jon laughed inappropriately as he read the details. "Looks like I'll get one more chance to bid farewell to old Captain Will. Yeah, a real shame." He laughed some more. "Couldn't have happened to a nicer guy."

24

K AT FLEW THROUGH the next few days working on a side project she had been awarded by the Plymouth Chamber of Commerce. Since her whale trip had been canceled, at least temporarily, she was working on a photo collaboration project with another freelancer to compile a series of Plymouth postcards that would be sold to the public. She loved historical photo projects, and this was a good diversion from the disturbing scene she had witnessed down at the pier.

She had spoken with Drew the day before and relayed all the information Ian had supplied during the meeting at the police station. He was glad to know the cops were continuing to keep an eye on their driveway, and Kat deliberately left out the part about her intention to attend Will Clarke's funeral the following day. To be truthful, she didn't really know why she felt the need to attend the ceremony at the cemetery, but she felt that at least she would be doing *something*.

Kat planned to arrive at the cemetery shortly before the service would begin and decided she would make at least a weak attempt to conceal her identity. She figured if she was in some kind of disguise, she could probably wander around pretty much unnoticed in the crowd. She laughed, thinking about donning the red wig she'd worn at a Halloween party years ago and the large, movie star sunglasses that would replace her usual Oakley's.

An hour later, Kat stood in front of her bedroom mirror while Dash provided the audience.

Her head was now a flowing red mane of wavy hair, dwarfing her features and making her look ridiculous enough to laugh out loud at herself.

"Hey Dash...what do ya think?!" She spun around and looked expectantly at the little guy stretched out on her floor, looking very perplexed. "The sunglasses will complete the look! This is pretty wild hair... Nobody will recognize me!" Dash groaned slightly and closed his eyes. "I'll be back later on," Kat said as she plumped up his bed and put on her bedazzled, tortoise shell sunglasses that nearly covered her face. "Wish me luck!" she hollered and out the door she went.

She arrived at the cemetery a little before the entourage was due to arrive for the ceremony. The area looked deserted, but she spotted the gravesite nearby, appearing ready for the upcoming service. Kat gathered her pocketbook and made sure to slip her small, Canon Elph camera inside *just in case.*

A true photographer, Kat rarely went anywhere without some type of camera to document her day. She checked to be sure her wig was on securely, glasses looked cool, and got out of the Jeep where she parked it down the curving road from the gravesite. She could see a long line of cars entering the cemetery, and she wandered out of sight as if looking at other graves. Walking casually around the cemetery, she kept her eyes on the area where everyone started convening for the Clarke burial. Soon, about fifty or sixty mourners were gathering around as if waiting for something to begin. Kat continued to stroll around the gravestones working her way toward the perimeter of the crowd, not quite sure who she was looking for, but not stopping to chat. She took stock of who she might recognize at the funeral. Most were strangers, but she recognized several faces of people she knew in town and made note that she didn't spot Patrick Walsh, the young man she had seen run out of the police station. Nobody seemed to recognize her, and she thought her disguise was working quite well. The Reverend arrived and soon the crowd huddled around the gravesite to hear the final words for Will Clarke. Kat stayed on the outside of the tight ring, trying to catch glimpses of most everyone who had shown up, from behind her dark glasses.

The burial service began, and the crowd hushed. Kat stood nearby and looked up into the large oak trees all around the cemetery then something caught her eye in the tree nearest the gravesite. She squinted her eyes through the large, showy sunglasses and thought she saw a rather unusual bird sitting on a limb, overhanging the gravesite from far above. She dipped down the sunglasses for a glance, and sure enough, she knew. Sitting majestically on the high limb was an owl. Kat was momentarily startled to see an owl in broad daylight, knowing they were generally nocturnal. Then, she felt a familiar current run down her spine and into her hands. They began to tingle. She stood and watched the beautiful raptor, who seemed to be tilting his head and looking down at her. The large, round eyes blinked, and his head turned at an unimaginable rotation as he continued to stare at her. The Reverend droned on.

In the moment, the owl looked at her, Kat instantly knew it was Mac. Usually, she spoke out loud to him, but wasn't able to this time because of where she was. In her head, she asked the question:

"Is that you, Mac?"

"Yes. Be careful today."

"How did you know I'd be here today? And how did you recognize me?"

"Kat, really?! I know these things. Stay aware."

"I intend to. We need to talk, to compare notes."

"We will. I have to go now. By the way, Dash let me know you were coming here."

With that final thought, the owl flapped its wings and glided off the branch and disappeared. Nobody else noticed him swooping between oak trees as he flew through the cemetery. Kat continued to stand silently at the edge of the crowd and watched him disappear high into the trees. The last part of Mac's message had caught her attention.

"Dash let him know I was coming here?? What the...?"

As the service ended, the crowd slowly dispersed, people mingled and stood talking as Kat continued to try to blend in. She saw various people approach the casket, throwing flowers on top. Most looked like friends or family of the Clarkes, and after a while, the crowd thinned and only a few groups of people remained. Kat slowly approached the gravesite as if in mourning and was shocked and startled when she looked down into the grave. Lying on top of the casket, among loose roses and carnations, was a small, round item. Thinking it was a large button, she leaned closer to see and gasped when she saw that it was a small, round piece of whale scrimshaw about the size of a quarter, etched with a whaling scene in black ink. Sitting right there, on top of the casket! What the hell was *that* doing there?!

Before Kat could process how that piece of scrimshaw got onto Will's casket, she felt somebody approaching behind her. She declined to turn around, but nearly stumbled into the grave when she heard a familiar voice.

"Good morning, Kat. Fancy meeting you here."

"Oh crap, thought Kat. It's Ian!!! How the hell did he know it was me?"

Kat turned slowly around and dipped down her sunglasses, quickly peering over them before pushing them back up. "Well, hello Detective Miller. Ummm, yes. It is a coincidence seeing you here. I guess you're wondering what I'm doing here?" Kat tried to sound innocent and official, but she could feel her wig slowly slipping down one side of her face. She could see Ian Miller stifle a laugh, and before he could answer, she grabbed his arm and pointed at the casket in the ground.

Ian leaned down. She heard him mutter an expletive and without looking at her, directed her to leave the area immediately and head directly home. Kat was not expecting this reaction from him, and he hadn't taken his eyes off the scrimshaw. He was studying the lone piece and took out his phone to snap a picture of where it lay. A uniformed officer came and stood behind Kat. He gently took her elbow.

He reiterated the command to please leave, and Kat silently obeyed. She turned and walked back to her Jeep. When she glanced back once, Ian was climbing down into Will Clarke's gravesite to retrieve the mysterious scrimshaw piece while several uniformed Plymouth Police stood silently by. He planned on claiming and identifying the second piece of stolen scrimshaw that mysteriously surfaced since Will Clarke's murder.

As Kat drove back to her house, all she could think about was how she now had more questions than answers to this whole mess.

Scrimshaw was stolen during the robbery, then showed up at the funeral. Somebody was leaving a trail of clues. And that somebody was apparently at the funeral! Now, she was even more convinced that the killer was dangerously close by. She needed answers from Ian about what, if anything, the physical evidence from the scene had shown so far. She'd not heard anything on the news or in the papers about fingerprints or any other serious leads. "Surely there must be something linking these events," she thought. "But what?"

25

K AT HAD JUST pulled into her driveway when her phone rang on the seat beside her. Shifting into park and picking it up, she saw the call was from Ian. She excitedly answered and felt a brief sense of relief that Ian was reaching out to her. Sitting there in her driveway, Ian quickly let her know he wasn't angry she had attended the funeral, but was concerned the killer might be attending as well. Since the Plymouth Police *were* sort of watching out for her safety, it wasn't the best choice to attend alone. He told her he'd spotted the red wig shortly after arriving and jokingly admitted he'd been quite impressed with the attempt at disguising herself.

Ian then went on in a more serious tone to tell Kat they had gotten results comparing all the fingerprints involved in the murder and the break-in, and remarkably, there were some common ones. Unfortunately, when they ran the prints through state and federal databases, there was no match. Apparently, their killer didn't have a prior criminal record or own a firearm legally. He also told Kat they had a list of people the department was processing to request DNA and fingerprint samples from. It was a time-consuming task, and progress was slow, but it could eventually match someone to the prints from both scenes. When Kat asked about the white bag belonging to Patrick Walsh, Ian reported that the bag had prints belonging to Patrick, as well as other sets of prints that matched prints found at both crime scenes. He said they were in the process of trying to lift even partial prints from the scrimshaw they had just found in the grave to see if they matched anything else they already had on file.

Kat thanked Ian for filling her in on his progress, promised not to over-step her safety net for the time being, and agreed to let the police know if she had any plans to be out alone for extended periods. She could sense Ian had more information that he wasn't revealing, but she knew that was how cases eventually got solved. After she had a chance to connect with Mac and compare notes, she felt certain that more pieces to this puzzle would fall into place.

After unlocking her front door and stepping into her home, Kat was in-stantly filled with a sense of security. Dash ran to greet her, wagging his tail madly and waiting for her to give him a petting or treat; either one would work! Kat indulged him with both.

Looking down at her happy little pup, Kat widened her eyes and looked directly at him with a questioning expression. In a soft voice she said, "Well Dash...it seems you were able to let Mac know exactly where I was going earlier today! So, how did that go down? I'm guessing you have your own link directly to him just like I do?! Hmmmm...I've got to think about that one for a minute."

Dash sat looking up at her with the hint of a dog smirk forming around his muzzle. Kat could have sworn she saw a slight twinkle in his amber eyes before he gave a little yip and ran off down the hallway. "Interesting," Kat muttered under her breath, making a mental note to ask Mac about the bond he now seemed to have directly with Dash in addition to her. *This* was a new revelation!

26

I AN MILLER SAT at his desk, staring at the whiteboard he set up in his office to keep track of important information when working on a case. The board was filled with post-it notes and names and lines connecting people, but none of it made sense. There were several people with possible motives, and many people with possible opportunity, to kill Will Clarke. He was slogging his way through the lengthy list of names of those who were voluntarily giving their prints to the police for possible matching. About half those asked so far had agreed to the process, and of course, the other half made up the list of the people more likely to be hiding something, thus deserving further investigation. Ian was in the process of getting court orders for the fingerprinting of those not doing so willingly. He had his eye on a couple of people in particular and hoped they would soon have some matches to the crime scene prints. Physical evidence was key in his investigation, but he still had to figure out who had the strongest motive to want Will dead. How the murder was committed was obviously to make some sort of statement. But what?

While Ian Miller was meticulously going over every clue he had to work with, Quinn MacIntyre was diligently working on the case as well, but using slightly different methods. Now existing in spirit and residing on the "other side," Mac was expanding his reputation as a talented painter to include sleuth work. He was excited to be working alongside Kat (and Dash) and in every case where they combined efforts to solve a mystery, he advanced, quietly, there on the other side. Achieving Angel status takes a long time.

Accordingly, and unbeknownst to Kat, she too was advancing on her soul purpose since her connection to Mac had opened. But this was a lesson she was just starting to learn.

Mac had been diligently following ancestry lines on the other side, pertaining to the Clarks' family tree, and discovered Will had many ties to the whaling industry. Generations previous included Will's great, great-grandfather, along with cousins and uncles, who went to sea as young men. The whaling industry was in full swing, as whale oil and other products from the grand beasts were in great demand. The Clarkes lost family members to the sea, but the ones who survived and returned home became part of the well-to-do circles that included merchants and ship owners. As Mac delved into finding some of these relatives and hearing their stories, he was slowly putting together information for Kat that might prove quite revealing. Tracking down particular spirits from the other side was usually an easy task for Mac, but this time he was having difficulty finding some whalemen whom he felt were key to answering the questions he had. Mac was sure they held the answers in their long-lost tales from the sea.

Analyzing the information he has uncovered so far, there might have been an ancient motive for the murder of Will Clarke this summer. Mac intended to fit the pieces together and hopefully provide Kat with information that would help solve the murder. Mac wanted to speak directly with Will Clarke and ask who had murdered him, but he knew there was always a delay when a person transitions to his side. His spirit would not be available immediately and Mac needed to be patient. Will would be busy now that he had arrived. Mac knew just who he needed to talk to, but finding them would be another story.

27

I AN MILLER WAS just shutting down his computer and getting ready to head home when he got a call from the front desk that someone was there to see him—if he was still available.

"Who is it?" Ian asked the officer at the front desk. "His name is Brian Buckley," replied the officer. "He says he has some information about the Clarke murder and something he'd like to turn over to you. He won't tell or show me what it is." Ian's interest spiked instantly. "Send him in. Let's see what this guy has to say, thanks."

After loosening his tie and momentarily stretching back in his chair, Ian felt the weight of the investigation starting to wear him down. He was tired and hungry, and tonight he wanted dinner and a cold beer. Maybe watch the Sox on TV before he fell asleep on the couch.

However, if this guy had some legitimate information, Ian knew he was down for listening to him and seeing what he had to offer. He could use a decent break in the case right about now.

Brian Buckley shuffled into Ian's office looking rather timid and somewhat stoned. He was tall and gangly, and Ian noticed not only his unkempt appearance, but the odor of alcohol emanating from him. Ian stood and introduced himself to Brian and motioned for him to take a seat across the desk from him. His first impression of Brian wasn't a good one, but Ian was anxious to hear what he had to say and had learned to let people talk before he started asking his own questions. Brian seemed nervous and had a bit of difficulty looking Ian directly in the eye for more than a second or two at a time, but he cleared his throat and said, "I found something down at the pier that I think you might want." He dug into his front pocket and pulled out a handful of change, and poked around for a second before extracting something and stretching out his flattened hand for Ian to see.

"Where and when exactly did you find this, Brian?" Ian gingerly took the piece of whale scrimshaw and turned it over and over, examining it closely. It had a whaling scene etched in ink on the front and initials in a fancy script on the back. He could clearly read the initials B.W. on the back. It was smooth and well-worn. It was obviously quite old and, obviously, part of the stolen items from the whaling museum. This made piece number three.

Brian mumbled something about seeing stolen scrimshaw pieces related to the murder on TV, so he decided to try and help by turning this piece in. He hesitated when Ian asked him if he had any other details that he might want to share with him after thanking him for coming forward with the scrimshaw. Brian shifted uneasily into his seat and looked around Ian's cluttered office before he continued. "Well, I found this at the pier down by the picnic table and trash cans over on the far side of the parking lot. It was on the ground, and it caught my eye. Then I saw on TV that you found a stolen piece, I thought this one might be stolen too." Ian hastily jotted down what Brian had told him. He was in the process of getting Brian's address and phone number for the ability to contact him again, if necessary, when Brian blurted out the best line Ian had heard all day. "I was also at the pier early on Saturday morning, before the murder. I saw who got on Captain Will's boat before he did or that lady did." Ian stared at Brian for a split second and grabbed his pen. Flipping open his notebook, he looked directly at him and nodded for him to continue.

"Why don't we start from the beginning. What time did you arrive at the pier?"

28

AROUND THE SAME time Ian was taking down the statement from Brian Buckley, who realized he had important input for the case, Mac was meeting and working his way through Will Clarke's list of ancestors who were involved in the whaling industry. Mac was sometimes amused, sometimes horrified, and sometimes didn't know quite what to think about the tales from the sea that these spirits shared with him. He found it all interesting, but not particularly helpful, until he was directed to meet with two men that a distant cousin of Will's had suggested he "look up."

Using the special method all spirits employ to connect, Mac set up a meeting with the men, who turned out to be brothers. For the first time since Will's death, Mac was gaining insight into the tumultuous life of a whaleman and how the Clarke family became notoriously intertwined with another family during that time. The ancient link between the Clarkes and the two brothers carried a centuries-old secret to the present day. Mac couldn't wait to interact with Kat and reveal what he had been told, and even more importantly, where she could direct the police to seek an answer to the question of both the murder and the robbery at the whaling museum. He was sure he (well, actually Kat) would be steering the police straight to a place where the truth would be revealed and the physical evidence supporting that truth would be indisputable. He knew the whole story now, and Kat needed to hear it, then let the police break the case. Mac chuckled to himself. He knew law enforcement would wonder how Kat knew where to lead them.

But at the end of the day, they wouldn't care how she knew, simply *that* she knew. It was time to let her know they needed to talk.

29

K AT STRETCHED OUT on the couch, watching TV and trying to keep her eyes open. She felt drained and tired, but wanted to stay awake to watch the news in case there was new information released about the murder. Dash rolled up at the end of the couch, twisted inside the soft throw they shared, looking content. The candle she lit when she turned off the lights was burning down, but gave off a warm glow that danced around the room.

"I'll just close my eyes for a minute or two and listen for the news to start," Kat murmured to Dash, who didn't respond back. Within ten minutes, both figures on the couch were fast asleep while the TV droned on. The candle eventually burned down and went out, the news came and went, and when Kat awoke with a start, she was disoriented for a moment before remembering she had been watching TV on the couch. Dash stood up and yawned in the dark, inching closer to Kat until he found her hand and began to poke her with his muzzle. Stroking his head gently, Kat clicked off the TV and lay quietly in the dark for a moment before attempting to get up and stumble upstairs to her bedroom. She could hear the clock in her kitchen ticking and the hum of her refrigerator in the dark, but all else in the house was quiet for the time being. Kat knew she would need to let Dash outside for a minute before she went to bed, but was still struggling to get up and move when she felt a slight tingle run up and down her spine and into her hands. Mac was apparently in the area. Kat knew he would manifest somewhere close to her, and her mind snapped awake at the thought of having the chance to connect with him. She hoped he had some information that might be helpful and maybe she could share it with Ian Miller. She found Ian seemed more willing to share information with her when she was offering information in return.

Sitting up in the dark, Kat gathered the throw tighter around her shoulders and waited. It didn't take long. Out of the corner of her eye, Kat caught a faint glint moving slowly around within her fireplace. There was no fire burning, but a small glow began to whirl in a circle, and tiny fiber optic-type lights joined together to form a loose image of a face. The face was undeniably Mac's.

Kat continued to stare into her empty fireplace, then she heard his voice. Well, she didn't actually *hear* it, but she heard it in her head, clear as a bell.

"Hello, Kat. How are you? I hope I didn't wake you..."

"Hi Mac! No, you didn't wake me, and I'm glad you're here. I've been anxious to meet with you to find out how you're coming along with the investigation on your side. So much has been happening, I can't wait to hear what you've learned." Kat pulled her covers closer still and waited.

The lightshow in the fireplace intensified and whirled faster, as if fueled by their ongoing conversation.

"Well, I am happy to report that I have solved your murder mystery. I discovered what the motive was, who the killer was, and the whole backstory, as you might say. I think you will find it quite interesting, as there was an unfinished tale between families that had endured nearly two centuries before ending here. Before you go to the police, you must first complete your investigation by following these instructions. I can direct you to the proof that you will need to convince the police who committed the murder and why."

Kat instantly felt her pulse quicken and leaned forward in the dark in anticipation, as if to ready herself for the reveal from Mac. Dash stood up and stared directly at the fireplace as well. It seemed as if they both were anticipating vital information. And Mac didn't disappoint.

Twenty minutes later, Kat and Dash both got up off the couch, stretched, and prepared to get ready for bed. Wordlessly, Kat snapped off the remaining lights and stepped onto her back deck before locking up. The backyard was cool and dark; the stars overhead streaked across the black velvety backdrop of sky. Deep in the woods, Kat could hear the tree frogs conversing and crickets gearing up for a symphony as the night grew still. Dash followed her outside and stood silently next to her as she folded her arms across her chest and shivered a little when a cool breeze rustled through the hemlocks. Somewhere close by, an owl called out and got a response. Kat stared up at the crescent moon shining above her and wished the entire murder investigation was over. The information Mac had passed onto her was swimming around inside her head, and she was trying to sort it all out and organize her thoughts. She knew the next day would be a busy one if everything fell into place as she hoped it would. Based on the details provided by Mac, she needed to arrive at the Plymouth Whaling Museum first thing in the morning to conduct her part of their investigation. If the information she was seeking was readily available, as Mac insisted it would be, the Plymouth Police could very well wrap up the murder investigation in the following days, with help from Kat (and Mac) of course.

Kat sighed and remembered that she had forgotten to call Drew that evening, but was now too tired to start a long conversation. She would fire off a quick text to say goodnight and tell him she had fallen asleep and would touch base tomorrow. She figured nothing would happen before she got to the Whaling Museum in the morning and hoped she would have a complete resolution to the mystery by the next time she talked with Drew.

"C'mon Dash. Time for bed." Kat shivered again as they came inside, carefully locking the door behind them. Settling in her cool bedroom, with a slice of moonlight appearing as a narrow triangle on her carpet next to the bed, Kat and Dash both fell into a sound sleep and remained that way until the moonlight turned into sunlight the following morning.

30

WHEN KAT AWOKE the next morning, she got up quickly and went straight into her kitchen to start the coffee. Dash stirred first and was now seated in the middle of the kitchen, so as not to be overlooked (as if that ever happened) or in case a tidbit fell his way. Sitting at the counter on a comfy stool with a steaming mug of hazelnut coffee, Kat got out her notebook, which held the information Mac had given her the evening before, and read over all her notes. She was anxious to get to the Museum early and start her research. She figured if it went as planned, she would contact Ian by the end of today with information she hoped he would want to hear.

Finishing her coffee and a light breakfast, Kat showered, dressed, and stuffed her portable camera into a tote bag and prepared to arrive at the Whaling Museum shortly after its opening.

She knew exactly what she was planning to look for. Mac's directions had been very specific. He was confident she would be able to find what was needed to help solve the murder and help Ian prove the killer's motive. From there, Mac believed the physical evidence would fall into place and the case would be solved. It seemed almost simple when she thought about it, but inside, she knew better. Nothing was ever as simple as it seemed.

The drive to the Plymouth Whaling Museum took Kat approximately fifteen minutes, and when she pulled into the parking lot of the stately-looking building with tall columns across its front veranda, she was in awe of the beautiful mansion as if it were her first time seeing it. The private sea captain's mansion had been purchased and transformed into a beautiful 21st century whaling museum, complete with furnishings and personal artifacts from the home's original owners. It boasted of several fine collections from prominent local whaling families and Kat never failed to recommend a visit to the museum when out-of-towners requested information on the local whaling history.

The curator of the museum had become a friend to Kat over the years. She had written stories and articles for the newspaper and photographed items pertaining to whaling, which the museum had graciously provided. Kat felt confident that once she arrived at the museum, her friend Rob Shockley would be happy to point her in the proper direction to find what she hoped would be the proof she was looking for.

"Mac...I sure hope you're right about this," Kat sighed to herself as she shifted her Jeep into park and pulled the keys from the ignition. She grabbed her tote bag and, with an anxious click of her key fob, locked the Jeep before heading across the expansive gravel parking lot toward the front entrance of the museum. Glancing around as she headed for the elaborate portico, she could only count about half a dozen cars in the museum lot. She wondered if Rob would be working on-site today, as she sure could use his expertise with her research. She felt bad about not contacting Ian first, but Mac was emphatic about her finding the information archived here first and foremost.

Kat reached the grand wooden doors carved in intricate detail and etched glass. The art depicted men in open boats, battling huge whales and thrashing about with harpoons while waves swelled around the fearful occupants. With a deliberate pull on the huge door, Kat entered the comfortably cool and dimly lit foyer to the museum. The air conditioner was humming quietly, and a young woman sat behind a large glass panel with an open window in front, working on a computer. She looked up and smiled when Kat approached the window.

"Good morning! Welcome to the Plymouth Whaling Museum! How can I help you today?" she beamed at Kat through the glass.

"Hello...I was wondering if Rob Shockley might be at the museum today and if I might be able to speak with him. My name is Kat Finley."

The perky attendant held up one finger to Kat and pushed a button on her reception panel. Within a few seconds, Kat heard Rob's voice through the glass partition answering her call. The receptionist spoke quietly into the phone, hung up, and buzzed Kat through a door, pointing to an office further down the hall.

"Rob's office is Room D, on the left. Have a nice day." Kat nodded a thank you and smiled, then scurried down the hall towards Rob's office.

Rob Shockley stood up when Kat entered his office, extended a friendly hand towards her, and motioned for her to take a seat. He was a soft-spoken and pleasant man, perfect for the museum, Kat thought, and was very knowledgeable about the local whaling history. She took out her notebook and looked gratefully at Rob when she asked for his expertise in locating three specific items at the museum. She explained, without mentioning Mac's influence, what she was hoping to achieve during her visit, with Rob's help of course.

"Thank you so much for taking the time to see me without prior notice today. I really appreciate it, Rob." Kat smiled and continued. "I sure hope you can help me."

"No problem, Kat, it's always nice to see you! I'm glad I was in my office. Now tell me, what exactly are you looking for today?"

Kat looked at the notes she had taken when she was talking to Mac, then looked hopefully at Rob. She handed him the list of dates and names.

"There are two specific logbooks from two different whaling ships that I would like to take a look at. There is also a personal correspondence in the form of a letter that should be with one of the ship's logs. The two ships are *Orion* and *Neptune,* both of which sailed out of New Bedford but were built locally. I have the voyages and dates I am interested in and hopefully, you can zero in on specifically which logbooks we need to locate. I know most of the whalers sailed on many different ships and voyages, so it's imperative that we get the logbook that pertains to one voyage in particular."

Rob looked thoughtful and absently tapped his pen while he was thinking. He swung his chair around to face his computer and typed for a moment before peering at Kat over the top. "I'm quite sure we have the logbooks for those voyages in our archives. You can absolutely look at them, but the bad news is they aren't at this location. We have many items stored at our off-site location, which is climate-controlled and has much nicer storage facilities. I'm sending a requisition over right now to have them pull what you're looking for, but it won't be delivered over here until tomorrow. If you don't mind coming back again in the morning, I can set you up at a private table in a conference room and you can research to your heart's content."

Kat was super disappointed that she couldn't get additional information today, but smiled and thanked Rob several times for his attentiveness, promising to return the following morning.

She drove home slowly, trying to decide whether or not to contact Ian Miller when she got home. Maybe sending him a quick text to say she had some information she was following up on might pique his interest and stall for time until she could return to the museum the following day.

Arriving back home, Kat sat in her driveway for a minute before going into the house. She was still debating whether to text Ian; it had been days since they had spoken, and she really didn't have any solid information to pass on yet. "Oh, the heck with it. I'll just send him a quick text to keep the lines of communication open," Kat thought to herself. Pausing for just a moment to think about her choice of words, Kat fired off a text that told Ian she had a potential lead for him, but needed some information from the museum to solidify its validity. She re-read the message and hoped Ian wasn't annoyed that she didn't call and talk with him about the potential lead directly. Kat realized this would have been the best path to take, but since her information was flowing from Mac, she had to process it and rewrap it before presenting it to anyone else. She hit send and waited to see if she got a response before getting out of her Jeep.

Ping. She got a text message back: ***things heating up. got major break. starting search. Stay safe & keep me in the loop. CALL if you have solid info leave msg if im not avail. will call u bk.***

"Well, ok. At least he doesn't sound ticked off. He also doesn't sound overly interested. I wonder what he's found out on his end? Hmmm… maybe that will all change by tomorrow."

Kat re-read his text, hopped out of the Jeep, and headed back into the safety of her home. She hoped the information she uncovered the next day would be a game changer for Ian if he didn't solve the murder in the meantime.

31

AFTER ARRIVING HOME from the museum, Kat went into her house and could instantly tell Dash was not himself. He ran in circles around her and danced on his hind legs while she bent to pet him and finally scooped him up into her arms. He wiggled happily and licked her face as if she had been gone for a long time, and Kat had no idea why he was acting so animated. He followed her from room to room, so as not to let her out of his sight, and she nearly tripped over him as he crowded her in his attempt to stay within inches of her feet. When she sat on the couch, he hopped up and plastered himself against her leg. Not sure what was going on, Kat dismissed it by flipping open her laptop and propping herself against a big pillow before scrolling aimlessly.

Searching for information pertaining to whaling ship logbooks proved valuable for Kat. She learned that the logs were generally written by the Chief mate and contained information such as the location of the vessel, the daily activities of the crew, most certainly the weather, and any whales spotted or captured. This was excellent to know, and Kat felt hopeful that if she could recover the correct logbooks from the museum tomorrow, most of her questions could be answered. She also discovered that crew members often kept their own personal journals that chronicled life aboard the vessel and recounted whaling adventures. These journals sometimes included handwritten letters, both received from home and written to those families thousands of miles away, awaiting the return of their loved ones to dry land.

Mac had specified to Kat a particular letter that she was to look for the following day. During their conversation, he revealed the letter would be hidden inside the logbook of the vessel *Orion,* tucked tightly inside pages that had not been opened in well over a hundred years. Locating the letter would be crucial to their investigation, Kat inferred from what Mac relayed to her. It seemed the information detailed inside the logbook and the letter would have to wait until tomorrow, and Kat was more than a little anxious to get her hands on them both.

The following morning, Kat got up, had a snack, and gulped down a cup of coffee before feeding Dash and getting ready to leave for the museum again. After finishing his breakfast, Dash went outside for a spin around the backyard, and Kat let him back in before getting ready to lock up and depart. As he had been the day before, Dash seemed anxious and was following Kat around as if he wanted to accompany her and not be left behind.

"What's up, little guy?" Kat bent down and rubbed behind his ears. He stared right at her, made a small yip, and sat down. "What?" Kat asked again. She had no clue as to why he was acting so clingy and felt bad that she couldn't take him with her. She knew it would be inappropriate for him to go to the museum regardless of how well he behaved, and she would never leave him unattended in her Jeep for an extended period. "I'm so sorry buddy...I can't take you with me this trip. How about we go for a walk on the beach after I get home?" Dash continued to stare at her then slowly retreated to his bed near the sunny window and curled up, continuing to watch every move she made. Kat slipped him a small treat and with a quick pat on his head she took off for the museum.

Her tote bag with her camera and notebook were on the front seat beside her and she absently flipped on the radio while she waited at a traffic light enroute to meet Rob Shockley at the museum. The local news came on and the newsperson read a short blurb from the Plymouth Police with an update on the murder. The newest information released by the police was to alert the public that the Plymouth Police now had a strong suspect in mind for the murder and robbery but would release the name and details later that day. They went on to say that law enforcement was currently seeking to implement all points bulletins on the person as well, probably within the next twenty-four hours. It hinted that the suspect was currently not in custody and perhaps unable to be located at this time. The news alert concluded with the fact that the local community might be instrumental in helping to locate the suspect. More updates would follow throughout the day.

"Oh my gosh," Kat mumbled to herself as she pulled into the gravel parking lot and skidded to a halt. She was wondering what Ian was in the middle of and wanted to get her information from the museum as quickly as possible so that she could update him with her discoveries.

Scurrying across the parking lot and ducking inside the heavy wood doors, the blast of cool air hit her as she entered the quiet building. She was pleased to see Rob Shockley waiting just inside the reception area with the woman at the front desk when Kat approached. He greeted her warmly then ushered her through and they headed down the hall toward his office. Once inside, he turned to Kat and as he grabbed a key to the conference room further down the hall, he said "I'm sorry you had to come back today to see the items Kat. I'm glad it still worked out for you. Strangely enough, I found out after I submitted my requisition yesterday for your items to be brought up from the archive room, that someone else had requested to view the exact same logbooks several weeks ago! However, the guy working down there who physically locates the stuff, told me the person who put in the request never showed up to look at any of it. He waited several days and didn't hear from them again, so he put the logbooks back and was able to retrieve them quickly for me today because of that." Kat had to stop for a moment when Rob relayed this to her. Quickly processing this information meant that someone else was seeking the same information that Kat was seeking. But who? And why?

"Who was it, Rob? Do you have a name?" Kat could scarcely contain her excitement.

Rob went behind his desk and pulled a sticky note off his computer screen. Squinting at the handwritten note, he read aloud the name. Kat was silent. *What?* It took her several beats to regain her composure in front of Rob. The first name meant nothing, but the last name was surprisingly on the list of people Mac had instructed her to research. Would their name mean anything to Ian?

Kat had no clue that in very short order, she would answer her own question and was on the verge of becoming very familiar with the name Rob had just given her. It would indeed become important to Ian Miller. If it wasn't already.

32

ROB SET KAT up in the conference room and brought in a lidded cardboard box containing the items she had requested. He gave her a pair of gloves to wear while handling everything, and she settled down at the long table with the first logbook Mac had instructed her to obtain. Rob showed her how to handle the books properly so as not to harm them, and she readied her camera and notebook in order to proceed. Her heart pounded as she gingerly opened the cover to the old, worn ship's logbook. The first page was decorated in a fancy script with hand-drawn whales beneath the ship's name, which stood out in a proud banner drawn in the center of the first page.

Orion had been elaborately scribed in black ink, and the date 1840 had been added as well. Carefully turning the page, information about the voyage had been thoughtfully written in a flourishing, swirling script which belied the lack of education most of the sailors possessed. The beautiful handwriting went on to list information about the captain, the various crew members, and their ranks, plus their financial standing while on board the vessel and throughout the voyage. Halfway down the list of crew members, Kat spotted three men listed with a common surname. Related, perhaps brothers? Checking her notes from Mac, she was shocked to see they were undeniably on the research list. No other designations were listed for those three. She needed to find out more. The surprising thing Kat made note of was the fact that their last name matched the last name Rob had printed out on the sticky note. Had she just found a nearly two-hundred-year-old link?

The person who wanted to see the logbooks before Kat requested them, but never showed up. She felt her pulse quicken. Kat kept reading. The information conveyed that the ship was originally built in Acushnet, MA, and had gone on seven previous voyages prior to the voyage about which Kat was interested in reading. According to Mac's information, the logbook she found described the whalemen on their trip from New Bedford, MA, to San Francisco, CA. From northern California waters, they would continue onward toward the Arctic Circle where they would spend the winter before making the trip in reverse and arriving home to Massachusetts. Kat started to read the beginning pages of what the meticulous Chief Mate had written and was captivated from the very first entry. Far north in the frigid waters the hearty whalers would arrive at Pauline Cove off Herschel Island. The area was within the boundaries of Canada's Northwest Territory. This meeting spot was a protected cove where the whaling ships would huddle together at the start of winter, kept warm by stoves on their decks and roofs overhead built to protect them from the elements. The natives living on the island would appear on the waterfront scene and for the winter months their families set up camp and joined the whalers in a community type setting where all would coexist peacefully.

The first hour flew by as Kat poured over the logbook, page by page, searching for another mention of the two men. Carefully turning each page and reading the details provided on a daily basis from the Chief Mate was fascinating and Kat found herself immersed in the daily life and grammar of the period. Crew activities, weather, and specific whaling trips were detailed without fail, every day regardless of the level of activity involved. Many days were described in a single entry when the weather, lack of whales, and therefore lack of excitement created spans of time where cleaning the ship and carving scrimshaws were the highlights of the day. Kat focused when the Chief Mate made mention of the growing tensions between two crew members and the "rowdy behavior and misconduct" that they constantly had to break up. By all accounts, it seemed as if most of the crew had eventually taken up sides with one man or the other and discontent among the men had started to fester. "Hmmm...not too different from today's corporate jungle atmosphere," Kat thought to herself. "Just in a different type of cubicle."

Kat was immersed in the logbook's stories of hunting down and killing whales, raging storms while at sea, and hostile interactions with other whaling ships. She learned many of the crew came from nefarious and questionable backgrounds and others were just decent citizens looking for a way to make a living for their families. Oftentimes, the two classes of people did not mix well on board. After the voyage was over, the captain and the agent, or owner, of the ship were generally the most profitable, while the crew barely made enough money to last until their next trip out. The finely built homes along the shore and prestigious land acquisitions were reserved mainly for the wealthy vessel owners or agents and those captains who made it home safely. The whaling industry brought great financial gain to those who invested in its future. The discovery of petroleum and the decline in the need for whale oil contributed in part to the end of the booming whaling era as they knew it.

Slowly working her way through the journal, Kat became immersed in the world on board the whaling ship. Stopping only for a quick break now and then, she proceeded to try and decipher every page she could. Finally, about halfway through the book, Kat came upon an entry dated 19 September 1840/Pacific Ocean. The author of the entry had hand-drawn a large whale with a harpoon alongside it in the margin of the journal. Not many of the entries had contained artwork on the pages thus far, so this particular day's account caught Kat's eye. Dark clouds had been drawn in the margins, and lightning bolts zig-zagged across the bottom of the journal page, indicating foul weather on that day.

For three days, the entries were brief, and the drawings of thunder clouds and lightning continued across the pages. Apparently, the Chief Mate had tired of the nasty weather and had resorted to descriptive drawings instead of a handwritten account of each day. On the fourth day, he had a different story to tell. And there were no pictures.

33

THE ENTRY DATED 19 September 1840 was of average length and yielded a description of a scenario they had encountered while on the voyage. Slowly deciphering the showy script, a sketchily described incident gradually emerged that chronicled a fateful day while chasing a huge whale in the northern Pacific Ocean. Kat read the log entry, then sat back in her chair and closed her eyes. The words were still swimming across the back of her eyelids, and her mind was trying to process what she had just read. Rubbing her tired eyes, then squinting to re-read the mesmerizing account of the disastrous day and the subsequent tragedy, she struggled to connect the dots between that day on the swirling ocean waves and a murder in modern-day Plymouth Harbor. The first things that jumped out as Kat continued to read were the names of those involved that fateful day. There was clearly a link to the present. The person seeking to read the logbooks at the museum had the same last name as three of the men on the whaling ship *Orion*. However, according to the entry that day in 1840, only two of them returned home to Massachusetts.

Kat got up from the table and stretched her achy muscles after sitting for so long. She could hear her stomach growling and, after checking her watch, realized it was nearing 1 pm and she hadn't eaten lunch. Just as she was deciding where to go and grab a quick sandwich before returning to the museum, there was a light knock on the door. Rob Shockley slowly opened the door, poked his head in, and grinned at Kat. "Hey, just checking to see how you're doing in here! It's been awfully quiet!" Kat laughed and, while she continued her stretching routine, told Rob that she was probably going to go out for a quick bite, then come back after lunch.

"Well, I don't want to interrupt anything you're doing, but I got a delivery a few minutes ago from the archive building, and they had forgotten to put this in the carton with the logbooks for you." He held up a worn manilla envelope held shut with one of the old-style clasps, using twine that twisted around the circular tab closure.

"Oh great! I wonder what it is?" Kat took the envelope and put it on the table, and briefly debated opening it right on the spot, but decided to wait until she finished lunch and then deal with it on a full stomach. Her curiosity was almost too much so she picked up her stuff, gathered her tote bag, and turned to Rob. "Let's go. I desperately need lunch! I'm starving! My treat!" Rob locked the conference room door behind them, and they left for a quick trip to The Rock, an authentic fishing shanty with take-out food located right down on the Plymouth waterfront.

Kat couldn't wait to get her hands on one of the best lobster rolls in town.

34

AT AND ROB returned to the museum after lunch and Kat settled back into the conference room to read the last logbook entry again. She often had to read the entries several times to understand them due to poor spelling, combined with unfamiliar whaling terminology. But this one had a very clear message, which Kat had no problem deciphering.

19 September 1840/ Pacific Ocean /
45 deg. N lat x 165 deg. W long
thunderstorms/high winds hvy fog & lightning
Poor vizibility/ 7' swells/hevy wind & 39- degree water
temp/ today was day #4 same weather
65-70 ft humpback whale spotted SE follow for day 7hrs./
6 mi under siege/ at point of taking whale approch by ship
port side through fog no signals
Apprched by bark Neptune in hvy swells/ Collid-
ed with her bow. lines entangled both crews fought to
gain control of beast and in process of melee rogue wave
crashed overboth bows
In hvy fog 1 sailor unintendedly pulled into ocean with
ropes. Apprnt. Drown. Unsaveable.
Whale recoverd By bark Neptune at end of dispute. Orion
crew returned one man missingdrownded/presumed dead

No whale recoverd /three lines lost total
Missing Orion crew member name added to Lost List at
end of logbook pg 252 with others lost/dyed on voyage

Kat sat back in her chair and took off her reading glasses. Rubbing her eyes from the strain and imagining the scene as depicted in the revealing entry. Fighting whales, torrential rain, fog, and lightning, and the result had been what? A man overboard? Who was it? "I can't believe they didn't even list the poor guy's name!" Kat muttered to herself. "I guess he didn't rate a personal shout out when he drowned...I wonder who the hell it was?"

Flipping toward the end of the logbook to page 252, Kat scanned down the list of names, which numbered 7 in total. Listed as number 4, on 19th September 1840, was the missing crew member's name.

Benjamin Woodworth age 22.

As Kat sat digesting this bit of information, she suddenly remembered that she had forgotten to look at what Rob had brought to her in the manila envelope before they left for lunch.

Untwisting the red string that wrapped around the circular button and opening the flap, Kat felt a rush of emotion flood through her when she reached inside and withdrew a stained and neatly folded two-page handwritten letter. "Oh my God! This is incredible!" Kat's hands began to subtly tingle and shake as she started to read the letter written nearly two hundred years earlier.

35

21 Sept. 1840

DEAREST MOTHER,
It is with tremendous sadness that I write to you of my expedition since departing San Francisco. I wish with all my heart that I did not have to pen this letter to you, and I pray it shall reach you more quickly than my last correspondence.

Several days ago, whilst engaging in the chase of an extremely large and violent humpback whale, our vessel encountered a violent storm with lightning and heaving winds. Giant waves crashed over the bow while we tried with great vigor to stop the huge beast from thrashing and entangling our longboat in the lines. We could scarcely see through the rain and fog while the wind howled about. It seemed our boat had broken apart near the bow due to the massive waves. We felt a rush of hope when another whaling ship appeared through the thick fog. We waved and hollered frantically as they approached because we recognized the ship and thought, finally ! Aid has arrived ! The crashing noise from lightning strikes and thunder were deafening as the waves raged against our boat and the whale continued to flail about.

After harpooning the beast, there was confusion in the fog, and the bow of Neptune hit our bow and caused wood to break and water to rush inside. A giant wave swelled and crashed into both vessels. Men from both the ships were yelling and fighting, and it seemed they wanted to lay claim to our whale. Whilst this was taking place, Ben and I held fast to our lines and firm against the wind, but the giant wave toppled Ben over when he stood for a better foothold, and a line thrown from the other boat wrapped around his leg. Ben was pulled into the dark water before my eyes. I was yelling for help, and through the fog, I saw Mr. Thomas Clarke, who I knew for true fact to be from the Neptune, holding the other end of the line wrapped around Ben's leg. I grabbed for him just as he was pulled into the waves by Thom Clarke on the other end, and I watched as my only brother disappeared into the waves and fog with the rope tangled around his legs. The last thing I saw was his woolen cap swirling out of sight. Thom Clarke stood in the fog on his bow and watched as well. When the fog opened up again, Thom Clarke was gone, and so was Ben.

We lost our feud with the whale after heroic efforts and many hours, before the crew from Neptune succeeded in hauling her in for their own gains. Our beloved Ben is gone, and the heathen Thomas Clarke could have saved him. I fear the sorrow and anger I carry inside me and vow that the Clarke family will someday pay the price for killing my brother. I shall seek out the wharf rat as soon as we are returned to port. I have knowledge that the Clarke family has relocated to Plymouth. Trust in the fact that I will make certain to locate them upon my return and seek my revenge.

An eye for an eye is God's will. I shall await your response, and dear Mother, please convey my sadness to Father, Abbie, and Victoria at losing Ben and missing my younger siblings as well. I trust Cousin Eli, and I shall return home next Summer and hope to find you all in good health.

With Love and Sadness, I remain,
Your Son, Lincoln Woodworth II

"Wow." Kat didn't know what else to say. Reading the letter Lincoln Woodworth sent to his mother explained a lot more than the Chief Mate's entry in Orion's logbook. A different version of the fateful day was documented, and the letter explained the reason for the hostile and adversarial feelings that brewed between the Clarke and Woodworth families. But who had known those ill feelings had festered for nearly two centuries, and the quest for revenge never faded away? It was all making sense now. Kat felt her hands begin to tingle even stronger than before, and she knew what that meant.

Usually, when Mac wanted to appear, her physical sensations became stronger, and Kat could sense when Mac was close by. But sitting in a small, mostly grey conference room and looking around, she couldn't imagine where he might manifest within these tiny quarters. She didn't have to wait long before she could "hear" him in her head, the same way she usually could, but there was no physical sign of his presence. Only his voice.

"Hello, Kat...yes, it's Mac. I know you can't see me anywhere in here...there was no real place for me to appear, so I'm contacting you strictly through thought. You read the letter, and it explains what happened nearly two hundred years ago, and it explains why the Woodworth family sought revenge on the Clarke family. You must get in touch with your detective friend immediately to let him know what you have learned. Also, you must be very careful after leaving here, as your murder suspect is currently on the run and is the very same man who attempted to retrieve the letter and logbooks before you did. Please proceed with caution, and I will contact you again soon. I will explain all the information that I've discovered on my side. For now, you have enough details to give the police a motive and Mr. Woodworth's name to follow up with. Stay safe, Kat."

The tingling subsided in Kat's hands, and she sat motionless for a moment, digesting what Mac had just relayed to her. Grabbing her phone, she fired off a text to Ian just as Mac had suggested.

" Quite sure I discov. motive. Long story. Jonathan Woodworth #1 sus. Find him. Call me when you can.. will fill u in." She hit send and waited. Picking up her camera, she began taking pictures of the front and back of the Woodworth family letter and pages of the logbook that detailed the 19th of September 1840. Within a minute or two, she received a text back from Ian:

"APB on Woodworth currently, unable to locate. tip from witness

matched prints. he ran. Details when we talk. Will call you later. Stay safe until Woodworth is located."

Kat felt a wave of relief wash over her as she sat alone in the stuffy room with the old logbooks and worn letter on the table before her. Looking at them, she could almost feel the energy each item emitted as it told its story to whoever cared to listen. Reading the letter between the young sailor and his mother, Kat could feel the love and sadness from hundreds of years before floating off the paper and surrounding her where she sat. The loss of her son, that in actuality was a murder, which could have been prevented, must have been overwhelming to their entire family. The old saying "revenge is a dish best served cold" seemed to have been their family motto. Seeking revenge two centuries later was hard to imagine but apparently the Woodworth family had passed the grudge down from generation to generation. Maybe the poor Clarke family in 2024 never even had a clue there was revenge to be sought.

Kat closed the logbooks, gathered the items neatly back into the carton, and slipped out to let Rob know she was ready to leave. She had taken pictures of all the vital information she hoped would be helpful to Ian. She thanked Rob, gathered her tote bag, and left the time cocoon of the museum and headed home. She didn't forget to look all around the parking lot area while walking to her car. Just in case that Woodworth guy is hanging around Plymouth. She hoped he wasn't. She just wanted to get home and sit tight until she could talk to Ian. She also knew after that conversation that she would need to get in touch with Drew to bring him up to speed with all that's happened since they last chatted. She might even fill in some of the details she may have left out during that last conversation. Or not.

36

KAT ARRIVED HOME and, as usual, Dash was more than happy to play meet and greet, then roll happily on the floor when she came through the front door. She locked it behind her and made a mental note to tell Drew that the Plymouth Police still had an unmarked car on the main street watching the end of their driveway. Kat felt safe and grateful that she and Ian were friends. She also couldn't wait to hear what he had to say about where they were in terms of solving the case. She had provided a motive and a name, and it seemed from the text he sent that he had luckily spoken to a witness in the meantime and somehow acquired prints from Jonathan Woodworth that matched the murder weapon or crime scene or both. Kat was secretly hoping that the information she and Mac provided would be instrumental in helping Ian solve the murder and the robbery. Mac was getting pretty good at "sleuthing" on the other side, and they worked well together. Too bad she couldn't tell Ian anything about Mac. But that was ok. She didn't really want to share him with anybody other than Drew and Dash. For now.

Kat let Dash out to run in the yard and stretched out in her recliner to rest for a few minutes. She had already had an eventful day so far and needed to take a few minutes to think about everything she had discovered at the museum. She had no idea what time Ian might call; she knew he was extremely busy and probably trying to track down Jonathan Woodworth right at this very moment. Filling her in on details was probably the furthest thing from his mind.

"Oh, c'mon Ian...call me!" Kat stared at her phone on the arm of the chair, willing it to ring.

"I'm dying to know what the hell is going on!" Kat reached for the remote to click on the news, and just as she picked it up, her phone rang, and she saw that it was Ian calling her back.

"Hey Kat...I have a few free minutes, so I wanted to give you a quick call and touch base. Can you tell me what you found out that you believe links Jonathan Woodworth to the murder and the robbery?" Ian sounded tired but interested in whatever Kat wanted to tell him.

"Thanks for calling me back, Ian. I know you're super busy, but I just wanted to pass on what I learned at the museum today. I think it provides a potentially viable motive, albeit a strange one. If you have physical evidence and some sort of witness, well, this could be what links him to the murder and robbery."

Kat could tell Ian was anxious to hear her news but wasn't revealing much from his end to her. She knew this was how it was dealing with cops, but she would pump him for more info if he wasn't more forthcoming before they hung up.

"Well, here's what I found out," Kat began. For the next ten minutes she had Ian's undivided attention to the story she unfolded about the logbooks and then the letter between the Woodworth family members. She had to leave out the parts about Mac's influence, but Ian didn't seem to question how she initially knew to even look for logbooks or letters. She told him about the two families and their whaling backgrounds that stretched into a current-day Hatfield and McCoy type of relationship with an 1840 murder being the motivating factor. She poured out all the details she had written down and then told Ian she took pictures of the logbook pages and the letter in case he needed to see them. For a long moment, there was silence on the other end until Kat heard Ian exhale a long sigh and simply say "Wow."

"Well, that explains a lot," Ian finally responded. "Now I get why Woodworth killed Will Clarke. It was a family thing. In his head he had to even the score. That's how the whalers did it." He paused and continued. "We had a witness come forward who was at the pier the morning Clarke was killed. He saw Woodworth board the boat before Clarke arrived, then saw him leave the boat right before you arrived. He didn't know a murder had been committed inside in the meantime, and that you'd be walking into a shocking scene. We got a warrant and went to Woodworth's condo in Duxbury, but he'd already made the jump. His boat is missing too. There's an APB out on him right now. We lifted his prints from his condo and made a definitive match to the murder weapon and the robbery scene. Hard to imagine, but that guy didn't even wear gloves! If only we'd had him in our database for something prior, we would have nailed him on this right away. So, it seems we have a strong motive and physical evidence linking our boy. It shouldn't be long now. We've just gotta find the creep."

Kat agreed, and Ian reminded her to keep her doors locked and stay vigilant until they were able to locate their suspect. "Thanks for keeping me in the loop, Ian. I know you can only reveal so much information to the general public, but I appreciate your keeping me safe and sharing information. I hope I've helped with what I told you earlier."

"Of course! What you've discovered answers some questions and raises others! We basically know why the two families had a hatred for each other, and that it went way back. I'm not too sure why Woodworth felt the need to knock off Clarke now, but their rivalry with their respective whaling tour boats probably didn't help."

Kat thought about this and agreed that one underlying issue could be the current struggle between the tour boats. Combined with a fierce, long-standing family code of honor among its whalemen, it's not unheard of for a feud between families to last generations. It just seems unfair that it ends with the death of a seemingly innocent young man just trying to continue his family heritage on the water.

Ian and Kat hung up after agreeing to keep their line of communication open, especially as far as the apprehension of Jonathan Woodworth was concerned. Kat knew she wouldn't rest until he had been caught, and this whole mess could be put to bed.

Next on her agenda, a talk with Mac, and later tonight, Drew. But for now, she and Dash needed a brisk walk on the beach. This case seemed to be coming to an end, but she still had a few loose threads that needed clearing up, and Mac was the only one who could help with that.

"Let's go, Dash!" Slipping him into his harness and snapping on his leash, they hopped into the Jeep. The hardtop was removed, and Dash was securely tethered in. Next stop: the beach.

Waving at the plain clothes cops continuing their surveillance from the main street, she and Dash let the breeze hit them straight in the face as they drove past, headed for the sun and the sand.

37

ETTLING DOWN ON her comfy couch with Dash tucked in beside her, Kat hoped she would hear something from Ian before the night was through. She had fallen asleep earlier after getting home from the beach with Dash and awoke with a start when he stirred first. She made dinner and sat on her back deck for a while, trying to read her newest mystery from Barnes & Noble, but she couldn't concentrate very well. She decided to go back inside to see what she could find on TV and text Drew. She had also hoped to hear from Mac, but after several failed attempts to connect at the beach and again when she got home, she opted to wait until he reached out to her. She'd learned that he always had a valid reason if he was unable to communicate back to her when she attempted from her side. Apparently, Mac was still very busy on the other side!

She texted Drew and let him know she had updates to pass on and that she thought the case was basically solved, except that the suspect was currently missing. She added that the police were still watching their house. She concluded with a heart emoji and **"Call me..will b up til 11pm pilgrim time,"** then hit send. The time difference made it somewhat inconvenient for both sides to talk in the evening, but since she'd had a nap earlier, she hoped she could stay awake until 11 pm. Maybe Drew would call well before that!

An hour or so later, while Kat was immersed in a sappy Hallmark movie, her phone buzzed, and Drew texted back saying he was free and for her to call him whenever she was ready. Shutting the TV off and grabbing a refill on her Pinot Grigio, she settled back down with her little shadow close by and called Drew. Dash stared at her during their entire conversation as though he were comprehending both sides and was part of it. She glanced at him several times as she relayed the latest information to Drew, and he appeared riveted to the conversation, watching her intently and blinking slowly as if he were understanding every word between them. Slightly unnerved, Kat continued describing her trip to the museum and discovering the logbooks and letter, thanks to Mac. Drew was fascinated with the apparent motive for both the murder and the robbery, and showed concern for the fact that their number one suspect was still at large. They discussed Kat's safety, and Dash seemed to almost nod in agreement. Winding down their conversation, Kat promised to keep Drew included in the updates. Then, she and Dash bid him goodnight. Kat felt as though Dash had energetically been very much a part of their conversation. More than usual. More than a typical dog.

"Well, that's just the weirdest thing," she said looking down at her little furry friend.

He simply stared back at her and blinked. But he understood every word.

38

THE EVENING PASSED uneventfully, and unfortunately, Kat received no further calls or texts from Ian. She went to bed with Dash close behind, and her first thought the next morning was about the case and what may have happened during the night.

While she made coffee, she wondered aloud if Jonathan Woodworth had been caught yet. She flipped on the TV while sipping her coffee and turned up the volume when she saw a snippet of an upcoming news story showing aerial footage of Plymouth Harbor and the surrounding area, with boats bobbing at their moorings below. Before the actual story came back on, Kat's phone buzzed. After turning down the TV volume again, she grabbed it and saw that it was a text from Ian.

"Woodworths boat found abandoned. Anchored off Clark's Island. Hes missing. Intrstng. item found on boat. Talk later. Stay safe."

Kat re-read the message, and just then, the news story came back on TV. She turned up the volume to hear the newscaster saying that the prime suspect in William Clarke's murder had been determined through DNA and fingerprinting, and police were currently searching for him. His tour boat, *Merlin,* had been found abandoned and anchored off Clark's Island near the Duxbury/Plymouth Bay area. Jonathan Woodworth was considered armed and dangerous, and the police requested any information leading to his whereabouts and/or apprehension. The news helicopter flew over Plymouth Harbor: Bug Light, then around toward the area where *Merlin* was still anchored. Kat saw the harbormaster, coast guard, and numerous state and local police boats surrounding the vessel and wondered if Ian were one of the men she saw swarming about the deck of the *Merlin* from the air. It sure looked as if it was crawling with cops at this point.

But where the hell was Jonathan Woodworth now? And what could Ian have found that he deemed "interesting" on his abandoned boat? "This mystery just keeps unraveling, Dash," Kat whispered as he continued to watch the news with her. "And I intend to keep digging until it's solved!"

Dash sighed contentedly, fully stretched out his front legs, then crossed them and looked back at Kat with that almost imperceptible dog smile. He blinked twice slowly, yawned widely, then patiently waited. He was no ordinary pup. He had learned to read the room.

Kat had a light breakfast, showered, and decided she would take Dash for a walk in the nearby conservation area that had recently opened new trails. She printed out a small map of the acreage showing the newly opened trails from the town's website, slipped Dash into his harness, and snapped on his leash. She grabbed a water bottle and her small camera, some identification, and her phone. After stuffing it all into a small knapsack, along with a snack pack of almonds with dried cranberries, they set out for their little adventure on foot. Cutting through the woods and the old cemetery next door to Kat's home, they respectfully made their way to the new trailhead through the old headstones, reaching the recently opened parcel of conservation land complete with a two-mile loop trail. Kat was excited to check out the trail as it was so close to her home, and she knew Dash would love exploring any unknown areas as well. The recently erected sign designated the proper direction to start the loop trail, and off they went.

Dash pulled his leash out as far as it would go and marched merrily ahead of Kat down the pine needle-covered trail. Deep woods lined both sides of the trail, and high above her head, Kat could see blue sky through the tops of the old, tall pine trees. A slight breeze rustled through the pines, and birds chattered loudly, hidden someplace in a thicket behind holly trees that had mysteriously sprouted in a small, sunny open space. The meandering trail widened at an open area next to an abandoned cranberry bog, where

Kat spotted two deer leaping over a section of an old stone wall that disappeared into a tangle of brush. Dash stopped in his tracks, watching them instantly disappear into the dense woods with great interest until he was sure they were gone for good. Kat enjoyed walking in the woods and usually stopped to take pictures of wildflowers or birds, or anything that caught her eye along the way.

After hiking for about half an hour or so, Kat stopped to dig her water bottle out of her knapsack and sat down on a large stump from a tree that had been cut down to create the trail. It made a perfect seat, so she crawled on top of the flat surface and dangled her legs over the edge while she sipped her water and nibbled on the snacks. Dash's leash was wrapped around a broken-off branch just in case he got the urge to bolt off; Kat didn't want to worry about him running into a coyote or fox or anything else that might potentially harm him or her as well. She kept a loud, piercing alert whistle in her knapsack and had to use it more than once to scare off a curious coyote that wandered in their direction while in the woods. Luckily, nothing larger than that had ever appeared during their walks.

Spotting a large, beautiful hawk of some kind, Kat watched it circle overhead, then silently swoop down in a grand semi-circle, and deftly land at the opposite end of the old stone wall the deer had jumped over, facing where Kat and Dash sat. They both stared, somewhat mesmerized by its majestic stature, with its wings folded at its sides but looking ready for flight at any moment. Its sharp, deadly talons gripping the edge of the stone wall and long, hooked beak made the raptor look rather ominous until Kat began to feel the familiar tingle in her hands and down her spine. Dash turned and looked at Kat. "Hey, wait! This was no ordinary hawk," Kat thought. "It's Mac!"

What she didn't know was that Dash already knew the bird of prey was Mac well before she did. In fact, Dash knew in advance that Mac was going to appear on their walk today. Mac had already told him.

Without a lot of preamble, Kat "heard" Mac quietly whisper her name and sensed he wanted to chat right there, in the middle of the woods.

"Hello, Kat. Yes, it's Mac, and I'm here with you and Dash today on the trail. That beautiful raptor you see...yep. That's me. Tough choice between the owl from

the other day and this hawk. I kind of like my wings. Now…to get to my point. How are you doing, Kat? Is your friend Ian progressing with the case?"

"Well, hello, Mac. Yes, I am ok! I like your wings as well. They seem to suit you somehow?! I believe Ian is moving forward with the case. He is still looking for Jon Woodworth. They found his abandoned boat, but he's missing. He texted me and told me he found something rather interesting on Jon's boat, but I don't know what it is yet. We haven't spoken. I can't imagine what it is."

"I do know what he found is yet another centuries-old link between the Clarke and Woodworth families. I believe in order to solve the mystery it creates, both families will need to pool their resources together and work as one to solve the dilemma. It may take time, and it may take some aid on my part as well. As always, I am at your service."

Kat laughed out loud at the gallantry of Mac's offer but continued in a more serious tone.

"I guess I will have to wait until I talk to Ian to get more information. I wanted to ask you, by the way, how did you know about the logbooks and letter were at the museum, and that they would basically provide the motive for the police?"

It was Mac's turn to chuckle. *"I have perfected some of my previous investigating techniques, and through my connections on this side, I was able to locate Benjamin and Lincoln Woodworth. They are the two brothers who were on the whaling ship, Orion, when Benjamin was pulled by Thomas Clarke from the vessel, Neptune, and into the ocean during the storm, leading to his drowning. His brother Lincoln told me that he watched Thomas Clarke knowingly pull Benjamin to his death, and he vowed in that moment to seek revenge on the Clarke family after his return home. He never located Thomas Clarke to repay him for the ultimate sin he had committed, therefore, his family was destined to carry the torch of revenge until Will Clarke's death. It took nearly two hundred years, but the score had been evened. Justice. An eye for an eye."*

"Wow. It's hard to believe the force for revenge could exist for so long. The will of those determined to seek justice never seemed to falter. Now poor, innocent Will Clarke is dead, Jonathan Woodworth is missing, and I hope the family feud is over. No more innocent people need to die. Mac, will the police ever find Jon Woodworth?"

"Well, Kat.... The police may find Mr. Woodworth, but he surely won't be answering any of their questions. You have it from good authority that he also won't be coming down for breakfast anytime soon. He's here. On this side. I don't presume to suggest how you'll convince your police friend Ian that you know he's undoubtedly deceased, but I'll leave that up to you."

Kat gave a little gasp at that revelation, and then there was a flapping motion. The regal hawk gently rose above the sunny, little clearing and circled one time overhead. He let out an eerie, echoing cry before disappearing out of sight.

Kat and Dash looked at each other for one long moment after watching Mac depart and turned to head home.

39

WHILE KAT AND Dash strolled leisurely through the woods, Ian Miller was deeply entrenched in the search for Jonathan Woodworth. He had received the initial call about a boat anchored in Duxbury Bay that appeared abandoned and matched the description of Woodworth's boat, *Merlin*. A harbormaster and Plymouth Police boat originally transported him to the vessel, which they boarded with guns drawn, but found no sign of their suspect. While waiting for the other law enforcement agencies to arrive, Ian scoured the boat extensively and one item immediately caught his attention while they searched for any clues that might be helpful in determining the whereabouts of Jon Woodworth.

Lying on the compact, combination galley table/desk, Ian spotted an old-style key, somewhat rusted, with a worn piece of ratty twine looped through its handle end and pulled tight into a knot so as not to become untied. It reminded him of the kind of key used in an old door, or maybe an armoire. It lay on top of a nautical chart of Cape Cod Bay, which had been rolled open, and two large, empty coffee mugs on opposite corners held it down flat. The key bore no markings, and Ian took pictures of the entire area, focusing on the rusty, out-of-place antique that had been left prominently in the middle of the table. The end with the twine tied to it was rather scrolled and ornate. Ian thought it looked hefty, like it might be heavier than an average key.

"Hmmm...wonder what that goes to?" Ian thought aloud. Continuing his walk through the small galley area, which was separate from and off-limits to the public, Ian made a mental note to retrieve the key on the way out and slip the unusual item into an evidence bag to bring back to the police station for further evaluation.

At first glance, nothing looked terribly out of place in the tight, private sitting area, somewhat hidden in the bowels of *Merlin.* The area sat below where the happy whale watchers above would squeal in delight, clutching their cameras and hanging off the sides of the railings to get a better look at the whales.

As additional law enforcement agencies arrived on Jonathan Woodworth's empty vessel and arrangements were made to tow it to another location for evidence processing, Ian pocketed the mysterious key and got a ride back to Plymouth Harbor. Sitting at the bow of the Harbormaster's Boston Whaler, the short ride allowed a stiff breeze to whip into his face as they skimmed across the open water, slowing down only when they entered the mooring areas. Ian couldn't help but wonder. What meaning, if any, might the key tucked into his pocket hold in this mystery? Also, where the hell was Jonathan Woodworth hiding?

Just when Ian thought he might get home early and have an evening to himself, his supervisor texted and asked him to call their office once he was back on land to update him on what he found on Jon's boat. Apparently, reporters were waiting for an update. Ian knew the key would create a whole other boatload of questions, and he could foresee a press field day regarding the most recent find on the killer's boat. Ian figured that if they displayed the old key on the TV and in the newspapers, perhaps somebody might recognize it or have some knowledge as to how it might be related to this case. Woodworth left it right out in the open on purpose. But why? Ian figured he would turn it over to his boss, and they could decide what to do with it. Right now, his main concern was still finding a murderer.

40

KAT SPENT SOME time running errands, and when she returned home, she clicked on the news while she prepared her dinner. She suddenly felt hungry, and after popping a frozen pizza in the oven and dishing out some leftover salad, she poured a glass of very chilled Sauvignon Blanc into a stemmed wineglass from Cape Cod Winery. Relaxing into her recliner, Dash was nestled on her lap within seconds, and they focused on the local news. It wasn't long before the reporters gathered all around the pier in Plymouth broadcasted the news that Woodworth's boat was found, but that no sign of him had surfaced. Speculation took over. The next segment showed a close-up of an antique-looking, skeleton type key. It looked rather chunky, somewhat rusty but still in decent shape, with some ratty twine or string tied through the looped handle end. The key looked to be approximately five to six inches long, and the newscaster didn't provide much more information except to say that the police were interested in talking with anyone who might recognize the key or have knowledge of its origin. They described how it had been found in the galley on the whale tour boat without any sign of the owner, the very same man police had issued an APB for days earlier.

"Huh," Kat said to her TV. "Now what the hell is *that* key for? Is that what Ian meant when he said he'd found something interesting? I wonder whose it is and what it has to do with this whole mess?" She took a long sip of her wine, stroking Dash's head while she pondered the surfacing of the old key. "Hopefully, Ian will keep me in the loop. I've got to tell him Jon is dead, but he's definitely going to wonder how I might have gotten *that* little tidbit of information. I guess I'll need to sleep on that one."

Later that evening, Kat and Drew chatted at length on the phone about what had been going on in both their worlds. Kat was thrilled to hear that Drew would probably be wrapping things up and heading home the following week, and she was relieved knowing the murder case had essentially been solved, except that the police didn't know that the missing suspect would most likely wash up on a local beach after a week or so of heavy surf and tidal changes. She hoped to talk with Ian the next day to ask about that key she saw on TV, and Drew was just as intrigued as she was about its meaning and origin. They signed off, and Kat and Dash crashed into their respective beds, falling into deep, dream filled sleep.

41

I AN MILLER SAT at his desk, twirling the heavy key around and around in his hands. His tired mind tried to find some rhyme or reason for its appearance at the last place Jon Woodworth probably was before he disappeared. All the usual procedures had been followed, such as tracking his phone usage, credit cards, etc., and so far, no activity had been detected. Where the hell was that S.O.B. hiding?

The key had been featured on the news, and pictures would be included in the local paper the following weekend. Ian knew it must have some significance to *somebody,* but who?

As he sat pondering his next move, the receptionist from the front desk came into his open office door and handed him a pink message note. "Sorry to bother. This call came in before you got here this morning. The woman said she wanted to talk to you about the key." She turned and disappeared down the hall as Ian looked at the message.

He had to read it twice when he saw the name of the person who wanted to talk with him: Pauline Clarke. Will Clarke's *mother*! "What the...how could she have info about the key from Woodworth's boat? He killed her son! Could there be *another* connection between these two families?" Ian couldn't call Pauline Clarke back quickly enough. What could she possibly know about a key belonging to the Woodworth family?

42

IAN CALLED PAULINE Clarke back and was shocked and perplexed after he heard what she had to tell him. After expressing his condolences for the loss of her son, she had an interesting story to relay. She had seen the news story about police finding the abandoned boat of her son's killer (information which she had been informed of before it had aired on the news), and when they showed the key on TV, she had a very strong sense that she knew what it might unlock. She went on to tell Ian that her grandparents owned a small chest, about the size of two shoe boxes, that had been in their family for several generations, ever since their whaling days. The chest had never been opened since they had owned it, and her grandfather told her mother that someone from the Woodworth family had stolen the key many decades before and kept it hidden in their own family for all these years. The chest had been passed down through several generations in their family. She wanted to take it to Ian's office and see if the key he found was the one that would finally open it. Pauline also mentioned that there was something stored inside the chest, as they could hear an item moving around inside when they shook it back and forth.

Ian's interest was piqued, and he set up an appointment later that day for her to come into the station and bring the chest with her. They would attempt to match the key to the lock, and maybe the Clarke family would discover what had been hidden inside for many, many decades.

Next on Ian's list, he needed to call Kat and bring her up to speed. He assumed she saw the key on the news like everybody else did, but since he still had no clue where Jon Woodworth was, he wanted to remind her to stay vigilant until he was caught.

Ian called Kat to fill her in and tell her that he had Will Clarke's mother, Pauline, arriving at 4 pm that afternoon with a potential mate to the skeleton key. Unfortunately, he still had no clue as to Jon Woodworth's whereabouts, and again, reminded her that he was still on the loose. When mentioning this last fact, Kat carefully expressed her doubt that Jon was still alive and suggested since his boat had been found, perhaps he had simply committed suicide and was not on the run after all. Of course, she knew for a fact that Jon was absolutely dead, as Mac had already confirmed his presence on the other side. But how could she convey that to Ian without sounding like some whoo-whoo, wacky, middle-aged nut? Ian pondered the idea of suicide and suggested time would tell if that were the case. Kat agreed, but held back from sharing any further opinions about the result of the search. She knew, in time, Jon's body would resurface somewhere nearby if he wasn't eaten by a shark first. For a brief moment, she thought it might be somewhat fitting on his final day for him to be eaten by an ocean predator, much like the demise of his unfortunate ancestor whaling on *Orion* in 1840. Strangely enough, history often *does* repeat itself.

Kat was totally caught off guard when she asked about the key and Ian relayed his conversation with Will's mother and her story about the small chest owned by their family. She couldn't imagine why the Clarke's would own a chest that the Woodworth's held the key to. It made no sense. Obviously one family had taken the key or the chest from the other. But why? And what could be hidden inside that Ian mentioned?

They signed off after Ian promised to let Kat know as soon as he was finished with Pauline Clarke's visit to the police station. He told her he was just as intrigued as she was with wanting to know what was inside the chest and why it was separated from its key so long ago. He hoped the Clarke family could provide some answers, and if they couldn't, his next stop would be visiting the Woodworth family again to see what insight they might have. He guessed that it all depended on what he found inside when they opened it. *If* they opened it.

43

PAULINE CLARKE ARRIVED at Plymouth Police Station promptly at 4 pm to meet with Ian Miller. Inside a reusable canvas shopping bag, she carried the ornate, wooden chest wrapped up in a towel. Ian met her in the lobby, ushered her into his office, and closed the door. Mrs. Clarke looked drawn and somewhat depressed after the senseless murder of her son, and Ian totally understood her demeanor. He thanked her again for coming in and motioned toward the bag she held in her lap. He took the key from the evidence bag and laid it on his desk. She sat across from him and carefully removed the anticipated item for Ian to see.

She withdrew a beautiful, wooden chest, approximately eighteen inches long with a curved top and dulled brass hardware, from the bag and put it on Ian's desk. He instantly picked it up and could feel something inside move as he turned the box over and over to examine it. The keyhole looked about the same size as the key, and Ian felt a rush of adrenaline as he picked up the key and gently tried to insert it into the ancient lock. It stuck for a moment as he tried to slowly turn it, and after a few attempts, it gently turned in a clockwise direction and clicked after it reached a full turn. Ian held his breath and reached for the top, gently trying to lift it open. There was resistance at first, then with a small creak, he peeled the rounded top back, and he and Pauline Clarke both peered into the blue velvet-lined chest. Pauline let out a small gasp, then covered her mouth and looked at Ian with questioning eyes.

"Oh my God. What is it?" she asked with true concern in her voice. Ian reached into the chest and gently withdrew a ten-inch, ancient-style fishing knife with an ornate scrimshaw handle and an ornery, rusty-looking blade on the other end. It had been loosely wrapped in a long piece of dirty flannel cloth. The handle looked about four inches long, and the blade of the knife was approximately six inches long. Ian turned the knife over and, on the backside, he saw quite plainly, the initials E.W. etched into the handle in heavy black ink and an outline of a whale drawn next to it. The scrimshaw etching was not well done, and Ian assumed it was a novice attempt by a bored whaleman.

He looked at Pauline Clarke and asked if she had ever seen or heard anything about the knife before today. The shocked woman looked blankly at Ian and simply said, "No. I have not."

"Well, it's hard to tell after all these years, but it looks like dried blood on this blade. It could be rust, but it's easy enough to identify. But why would a bloody knife be hidden inside a chest owned by you, and the key in someone else's possession? It makes no sense." Pauline continued to stare at the knife, not quite sure what to think about it being a part of her family's heirlooms. Ian's imagination, on the other hand, was racing with potential reasons for someone to hide a bloody knife in the family chest and then hide the key.

"Technically, this knife belongs to you, Mrs. Clarke. As an item inside the chest you own, it's yours now. The key, however, is part of the evidence we found on Jonathan Woodworth's vessel, so it must remain in the possession of the police until his trial is over. You are welcome to take this chest and the knife inside home with you. I'm not sure what their meaning is. I would suggest you leave the chest open, as you won't be able to unlock it again if you close it. If you prefer to leave the knife with me, perhaps we can contact our source at the Whaling Museum to do some research on its origin. It's more than a coincidence that your family and the Woodworth family seem to be linked by your ownership of these two items. Would you like me to keep the knife, or do you want to take it with you?"

Pauline Clarke looked at the knife and shuddered. "No. I don't want that thing in my house. You can keep it, give it to that museum guy, or do whatever you want to do with. It's fine by me. I'm done with connections to that dreadful Woodworth family." She picked up the wooden chest and carefully put it inside the tote bag, tilting it sideways to keep the lid open. "Thank you for your time, Detective Miller, and for opening this for me. We've wondered for years what was inside, and now we know. I almost wish we didn't have to tell you the truth. Have a nice evening, Detective."

Pauline Clarke left Ian's office. He sat at his desk, turning the knife over and over in his hands. He couldn't help but wonder what the initials etched into the handle stood for. E.W., plain as day. Could the W be for Woodworth? Why would it be inside a Clarke family chest? And, what the hell went on between these two families nearly two hundred years ago?

Ian's cell phone began to vibrate and ring on his desk. He snatched it up and listened without responding until the very end of the nearly one-sided conversation. "Yes. Thanks for letting me know. No, not surprised, really. I'll get back to you. Thanks again." Hanging up, Ian sighed loudly and rested his elbows on his desk while rubbing his temples. It was now official. The call had informed him that Jonathan Woodworth's body had washed up in the salt marsh along the coast of Sandwich. He had been positively identified by the medical examiner, and the body was now waiting in the morgue.

Ian took the news without surprise and completely forgot that Kat had suggested this particular outcome previously. Finding his body was a plus. It tied up the loose ends rather nicely, except for the part about the newly discovered bloody knife.

IAN DECIDED TO give Kat a quick call before heading home. He wanted to let her know Jon's body had been recovered, and apparently, suicide *had* been the reason for his disappearance. Next, he wanted to tell her about the knife he and Pauline Clarke discovered in the chest. He wanted to remember to mention the initials E.W., having been etched into the whalebone handle and the outline of a whale as well. Maybe it would mean something to her?

The conversation between Ian and Kat was brief, but it was long enough to raise new questions in Kat's mind about the long-standing relationship between the Woodworth and the Clarke families. When Ian mentioned the initials, Kat instantly remembered that she had read about three crewmen on *Orion* with the last name Woodworth. One was Benjamin, who died on the fateful day in September 1840. His brother, Lincoln, wrote the letter home to their mother, which Kat found inside the logbook outlining Ben's death on the seas that day. She also remembered seeing the name Eli in the letter Lincoln penned home, and he was referred to as "Cousin Eli." He must have been a cousin of the Woodworth brothers who accompanied them on their voyage. Kat and Ian discussed these family connections and circled back to the present day.

Benjamin Woodworth was killed by Thomas Clarke. Lincoln Woodworth returned home to seek revenge. What happened to their cousin, Eli Woodworth and who would have hidden a bloody knife with his initials on it inside a Clarke family trunk with a key that was in the possession of a Woodworth, their archrival? And why? Kat seriously wondered what the heck kind of connection these two families truly shared. Apparently, it was more bad than good! It seemed possible their twisted family history included more than just one murder at sea.

Kat suggested Ian bring the knife to Rob Shockley at the museum and see what kind of information he might uncover. He agreed there was nothing to lose by turning it over to the experts, and it wasn't as if it were a piece of evidence in the current murder investigation.

After they hung up, Kat sat back and put her feet up. Everything had turned out almost exactly the way Mac had predicted it would. She laughed out loud and sensed they would be connecting soon.

She couldn't wait to ask him about the knife. And what happened to Cousin Eli?

45

KAT HUNG UP from her call with Ian and couldn't help but smile to herself. She almost thought she saw Dash smiling too, but he marched away and stood at the door to be let out. Slipping out onto her back deck with Dash in the lead, she heard the birdsongs echoing across the yard and felt relieved that the case was essentially over. Leaning against the railing and watching Dash scamper back and forth across the yard, she decided that she needed to clear her head and a trip to the beach before dinner would be the perfect distraction.

Within a few minutes, they were sailing happily along in the topless Jeep while Kat sang loudly and off-key to a Steely Dan song on the radio. Dash was tethered into his harness on the front seat, looking rather pleased with the spontaneous beach trip.

He hoped it was low tide and that Kat would let him off his leash for a bit so he could run wildly along the sand, just out of reach from the incoming waves. Dash loved the beach almost as much as Kat did. He was also excited because Mac was going to be there. Kat didn't know it yet, but he was sure of it. He was the one who let Mac know that's where they were headed.

After kicking off her sneakers and letting Dash lead her across the warm sand towards the water, Kat couldn't help but feel invigorated and let the lingering sun remind her she still had almost a whole summer ahead. It hadn't been ruined entirely! The season had started with an unexpected shock, but there would be sunny times ahead. She'd make sure of it.

The beach was mostly deserted except for a young couple walking hundreds of yards away along the waterline, enjoying the flat expanse of sand at low tide. Kat unsnapped Dash from his leash and let him run in circles, happily splashing in the shallow pools and barking at approaching waves. Kat threw down her towel on a dry, sandy spot with minimal rocks and waded out into the shallow, gentle waves, headed towards shore. Standing knee deep in the slowly retreating and approaching waves, Kat spotted a school of fish darting past and a starfish partially embedded in the sand right next to her foot. As a wave rolled in, its fingers disappeared, and it tumbled away, towards the next stop along its underwater journey. The seagulls screeched overhead and did their best dives into the shallow pools, only to surface with a clam in their beak, which would be dropped onto the paved parking lot behind her for quick opening. The breeze was perfect, and Kat stood motionless as she looked out across the huge, blueish green ocean to where it met the sky. She wondered about the men and women who spent their whole lives at sea. Was it decided by choice or by necessity? She figured it was probably a little of both. Reading the logbooks describing the difficult life and daily adversities on board the whaling ship was enough to make Kat more than a little grateful for her life today.

Turning back to rest on her towel, she kept an eye on Dash and felt her tensions disappear with each retreating wave. The sun was behind her now and felt good on her back. Drew would be home next week, and hopefully their lives would get back to normal. (Again!) She had noticed the police detail camped near her driveway had finally been removed, and she felt relief about that. Things wouldn't appear so dire to Drew now that the cops were gone and the case was mostly over. She would try her best to downplay the whole thing, but she knew that he knew the truth.

Finding Will Clarke had scared her to death! All she had wanted was to simply go out on that whale watching tour! So much for the photoshoot. They were now down to one local whale watching company. Kat wondered if the Chamber of Commerce dared send her to try another photoshoot. With Patrick Walsh? The thought made her shudder.

Leaning back on her towel and watching the water slowly approaching, she called Dash over to dry him off, and they both sat mesmerized by the endless waves rolling towards them and gently disappearing when they hit the shore.

Kat felt the familiar tingle in her hands first. It then snaked its way down her spine as she sat on her towel in the afternoon sun. She knew this was the prelude to Mac appearing somewhere, but she wasn't quite sure where that might be, yet. Dash had snuggled in very close to her and appeared to be watching the water intently. Kat followed his gaze and was startled to see what appeared to be a face swirl by her in the tight curl of a small wave before it joined the sand and dissipated. Before she could let out a small gasp, another wave approached, and as she looked at its rising crest before it tumbled forward, she was positive she spotted the face of none other than Mac rushing by in a pool of seafoam. He appeared to be enjoying his wave surfing. Kat laughed when his face rolled by in the frothy, swirling surf a third time before disappearing into the sand again.

"Oh! Ok...so this is how you're coming through today...well hello!" Kat grinned as another Mac face tumbled by her, then disappeared as quickly as it had appeared. "How are you?!" Dash stared at where the face had just appeared, but there was nothing more than retreating water now.

"*Hello, Kat! I'm well. I trust you are feeling more relaxed now that the mystery has been solved. Isn't the beach beautiful today!*"

"Yes, it is! Dash and I love it here. Just out of curiosity, how did you know that we would be here?" Kat asked while stifling a small laugh. "Rather a coincidence, don't you think?"

"*Well, not exactly...*" Mac's shimmering image floated in a shallow tidal pool in front of Kat's towel. She sat staring at his watery face, amazed that she could recognize his distinctive features. They had become familiar to her after identifying him in so many family pictures over the years.

"*This is probably a good time to tell you that over the past year while we have been honing our communication skills with each other, I also opened a time passage that has existed between myself and Dash for many years. He is now included in my "earthly connections" contact list, just as you are. On this side, we all must create and work with one. He has become acutely aware of my energy, often times even before you are, and can let me know if he senses you could be in any danger. I can now transmit my thoughts to him as well. The three of us are connected. Dash told me you would be here at the beach, and I decided I needed a beach day so, well, here I am!"*

Kat pulled her knees up to her chest and wrapped her arms around them. This was a new revelation from Mac. She looked quizzically at Dash, who was sitting right next to her. He looked up, made definite eye contact, then returned his gaze back to the sea.

After a brief silence where Kat was digesting this information and wondering how it all had evolved, she asked Mac what this dynamic would mean for her and Dash, as far as their family was concerned. Was it ok for her to reveal to Drew that their dog has a special talent that included communicating with Spirit?

"You have nothing to worry about. And yes, it is fine for you to let Drew know that our little buddy here is more special than you knew. It won't affect your relationship with him. The main reason I've opened the time passage with him is that we have shared a long, happy relationship. You see, Dash used to be my dog when I was a young man. We were together here, on this side. Then it came time for him to reincarnate again. He chose to be your dog in this lifetime and now the three of us are linked. You might notice that Dash can sense my impending arrival long before you can. It's just part of the bond we created nearly two hundred years ago and now it has come full circle, and we are connected again. Dash has the special ability to let me know when you need my assistance and can keep me up to date on whatever I need to know. He is a very special little dog, and I am thrilled to connect with him again."

"Wow," replied Kat. Hearing that Dash had been Mac's dog many, many decades ago was fascinating! "So that's how you knew beforehand where I was going, and you showed up so we could communicate. And Dash was behind the scenes the whole time, keeping you in the loop!

I guess it's good to know you can keep an eye on me through my dog, or would that be *your* dog?!!"

"The other thing I wanted to reveal to you before you dip out again is what my friend Detective Miller found in the chest belonging to Pauline

Clarke's family. He told me that when they opened it, with the key he found on Jon Woodworth's boat, they discovered a bloody whaling knife with a scrimshaw handle and initials on it. The initials we E.W. We know it has nothing to do with the current murder, which you played a huge part in solving, by the way, but we don't know if it has any significance. Do you know anything about that knife?"

Mac's reflection in the tidal pool rippled a little, but Kat could distinguish a smile on his face as it shifted. *"Well....to tell you the truth...I actually do know a little something about it... but I'm not sure you want to go there with me today...,"* Mac responded.

Kat was curious, but didn't respond back. Her mind raced with the possibilities, but she waited for Mac to continue. Honestly, even *she* wasn't sure she wanted to go down this road if it was going to extend this mystery any further. She had the rest of her summer to enjoy!

After a long pause, Mac continued. *"While I was doing my investigation on this side for the murder of Captain Will Clarke, I obviously met members of both the Clarke and Woodworth families. Although the current murder was committed in retaliation for the murder committed back in the 1840s, I did discover that the long-standing feud between the two families previously existed before the whaling death of Benjamin Woodworth. Prior to their departure on the whaling vessel, members of the two families had brawled in the local pub and were asked to vacate the building. Once outside, one of the men pulled out a knife and at the end of the fight, Peter Clarke had been stabbed and died from his wounds. Rumor has it that Eli, who accompanied his cousins Lincoln and Benjamin Woodworth on their excursion, was the owner of the knife found near Peter Clarke's body. It had initials on it, but before the law arrived, somebody picked it up and disappeared with it. It had been hidden in that box since the day of the murder, and only the Woodworth family had the key. The problem was the box had been stolen over the years, obviously by a Clarke family member, but they had no way to open it once they had possession of it. Until your Detective friend brought the box and the key together, that knife would have stayed hidden for another hundred years. Somebody was looking for proof, and by the time it was discovered, it was too late. Somebody was trying to hide something, and somebody was trying to find something. All of the people involved have crossed over. It appears as though the secret has been revealed and confirmed today. That is what I discovered about the knife you inquired about."*

Kat continued sitting and staring at the shifting sand and water before her and tried to piece together the information Mac had just shared with her. Pauline Clarke had implied that somebody in the Woodworth family had stolen the key from their family, yet the flipside alleges that a Clarke family member stole the chest from the Woodworths! Who actually stole from whom? For a split second, Kat figured it really didn't matter. But her brain couldn't help but start to unravel the mystery. This had raised more questions!

"Do you think you could find out more information on your side?" Kat asked as she stared at Mac's face in the water.

She saw Mac smile again, *"Perhaps I already have...but that is a tale for a different beach day!"*

With that, a random wave rolled ashore and filled the tidal pool. Kat watched as Mac's image slowly disappeared, melting into the sand.

THE END

Acknowledgements

I want to express my gratitude to Kevin for hanging in there with me throughout this process. You're the best! Thanks for your unwavering support.

For more information, please visit:
Diannehuntsmith.com
Brileybaxterbooks.com

Titles in the *Eye in the Sky* Series:

Mystery at Chilmark
Whisper in the Waves: Murder in Plymouth Harbor
Look for book #3 soon!